WHEN SPARROWS FALL

When Sparrows Fall

Diana Blackstone

This is a work of fiction. Names, characters, places, and incidents either are the product of the author's imagination or are used fictitiously, and any resemblance to actual persons living or dead, business establishments, or events is entirely coincidental.

The publisher and author acknowledge the trademark status and trademark ownership of all trademarks and locations mentioned in this book. Trademarks and locations are not sponsored or endorsed by trademark owners.

When Sparrows Fall © 2015 by Diana Blackstone

All rights reserved. No part of this book may be used or reproduced in any manner whatsoever without written permission from Leap Books, LLC, except in the case of brief quotations embodied in critical articles or reviews.

Cover Art by Leap Books, LLC.
Interior Layout by NovelNinjutsu.com

Leap Books, LLC, P.O. Box 63, Otego, NY., 13825
www.LeapBks.com
Contact information: leapbks@gmail.com

First edition June 2015
ISBN: 978-1-61603-045-2
Published and printed in the United States of America.

For my mother, Thelma I. Blackstone
1944-2012
I miss you every day and can't wait to see you again.

Table of Contents

1: Starting Over……………………………...	1
2: First Day at School……………………..…	8
3: Provoke Not……………………………....	19
4: Mystery in the Dark………………………	27
5: A New Friend…………………………..…	33
6: Who's to Blame?...	40
7: Aunt Lydia………………………………..	52
8: When Sparrows Fall………………………	60
9: A Day of Surprises………………………..	67
10: On the Road……………………………..	74
11: Remembering……………………………	81
12: A Wedding………………………………	95
13: Rescue…………………………………....	106
14: The Kittens…………………………….....	116
15: Stormy Weather…………………………..	122
16: Sister Brubaker's Secret…………………..	131
17: Sneaking Out…………………………….	138
18: A New Arrival…………………………...	154
19: Unintended Consequences………………	159
20: Hope…………………………………….	175
21: Testing…………………………………..	180
22: Taking a Chance…………………………	187
23: The Passengers…………………………..	198
24: Four Months…………………………….	210
25: A Close Call……………………………..	219
26: Cover-up………………………………....	225

27: Trapped…………………………………	234
28: Reconciliation………………………....	241
29: The Letter……………………………..	245
Glossary and Discussion Guide……………..	253
Acknowledgments…………………………...	259
About Diana Blackstone…………………….	261

1
STARTING OVER

It was getting hard to breathe. A bead of sweat trickled down the back of my neck. I cracked the chiffarobe's door to get some fresh air.

"D-d-do y-you think i-i-it is over?" asked Amos.

"Shh." I pulled the door shut.

It had been quiet for a while. My heart no longer hammered inside my chest. My knees ached.

As huge as the closet appeared on the outside, it wasn't big enough to hide my little brother and me comfortably for long, even if he was only six.

My cousin Mary's scratchy wool coat, hanging next to me, brushed against my cheek.

I shoved it aside.

Soft footsteps approached. "You can come out now." Leon stood outside with little Magdalena's hand clutched in his. Uncle Jacob must have finally stormed out to the barn, leaving the rest of us behind to pick up the pieces of his rage.

Whenever Uncle Jacob flew into one of his tirades, I pulled Amos into the chiffarobe in the corner of my bedroom while eight-year-old Leon hid with Magdalena under his bed. From there he had a clear view down the stairs. When Leon saw Uncle Jacob leave through the back door, he would come to get Amos and me. That had been our routine for the past three months since Uncle Jacob had become our stepfather. So far, it had kept us safe.

We found our mother in the kitchen holding a wet cloth against my cousin Mary's reddened cheek as she sat at the maple table in the center of the room. Mary's bloodshot eyes and wet eyelashes revealed that she had been crying. An inviting fire crackled in the fireplace. The peaceful kitchen belied the anger that had filled it only minutes earlier.

"Why do you provoke him so?" I asked, irritated.

"Hush, Susanna." Mama wiped Mary's face. "It is not her fault."

Mary scowled at me.

"Well really, Mama, she ought to know by now when to quit arguing with him," I complained. "Why did you agree to marry such a man?"

Mary grimaced at me with narrowed, green eyes.

"*Abatz*. That is quite enough. Please put Magdalena to bed and then help me clear the table." Tears brimmed in Mama's eyes. She hastily brushed them away.

"Come, Magdalena." I took my baby sister's hand and led her to the bedroom she shared with Uncle Jacob and my mother. A lump caught in my throat. I hadn't meant to make Mama cry. Tears burned in my eyes as well. I already knew the answer to my question, anyway. My mother had been given little choice. The district's Mennonite bishop and church elders had seen to that.

A kerosene lamp glowed dimly on the bedside table. I unfastened the hooks and eyes on the back of Magdalena's dress and lifted it over her head. An unpleasant odor told me she had soiled her diaper again.

I looked forward to the day she wouldn't need diapers anymore. Then again, I'd miss her baby soft blond curls, chubby little legs, and the funny way she mispronounced words. I felt a sudden urge to hold her. I could have lost her, too, on the covered wagon trip from Pennsylvania that took the life of our father five months ago.

Magdalena squirmed in my arms. "Down," she whined.

I relaxed my tight embrace and set her down. "Fine. Now stop *rutsching* around and lie still. I need to clean you up." After changing her diaper, I dressed her in a warm nightgown to ward against the chilly March night, kissed her cheek, and tucked her into the crib in the corner of the room.

Even though her eyes were heavy with sleepiness, she whimpered when I turned toward the door.

"Shush now. No more *gretzing*, and I'll sing you one song." I sat in the wooden rocker next to the crib, reached through the slats to rub her back, and sang a German lullaby I'd learned from Grandma Clara during the two months we'd lived with her and Great Aunt Ann when we'd first arrived in Harrisonburg. Before I was done with the second verse, Magdalena was sound asleep.

By the time I returned to the kitchen, Mama and Mary had already cleared the table and washed the dishes. "You can go to bed, Mary. You have had a hard enough night as it is. Susanna can dry," Mama said.

Mary glowered as she tossed the dish towel to me and headed toward the stairs.

"I'm sorry, Mary." I worked my features into what I hoped would appear to be a sincere, apologetic expression. "I didn't intend to make you feel worse."

"Leave me be," she muttered without bothering to turn around.

When Mary's footsteps patted in the room we shared above the kitchen, I whispered, "Mama, I try. We simply don't get along. You heard me apologize, didn't you? Did you hear what she said to me? 'Leave me be.'"

"Be patient." Mama handed me a dripping bowl to dry. "Think about things from her point of view. She was the woman of the house for years before I married her papa. We must seem like unwelcome invaders to her. Not only that, but until we moved in, she could keep her pain private. Now we know firsthand how her papa treats her. She must feel humiliated."

"I know, I know. But it's been three months, and she has been nothing but nasty to me. I know Uncle Jacob is mean to her, but she could at least try a little harder to get along with him, couldn't she? She nags him about not eating enough, corrects him when he misquotes Scripture, and even forgot to shine his Sunday shoes two weeks in a row – "

Mama cut me off, quoting from the book of Matthew. "*Judge not, that ye be not judged.* Forgetting to shine his shoes does not warrant a beating. Nothing does. And you know how unpredictable his temper is. What prompts a beating one day is overlooked the next."

"Except when it comes to Peter – Uncle Jacob never ignores *his* mistakes," I replied, "and he's only eleven."

"I wish…well, we need to pray. We can at least do that."

I sighed in frustration. That was Mama's answer for anything troubling. Pray. What good did prayer do? Prayer didn't keep my papa from dying. Prayer didn't stop Uncle Jacob from yelling and hitting. I used to feel so close to God when I lived in Pennsylvania. He must have stayed behind.

"Where are the boys?" I asked.

"Amos went to bed. I sent Leon to help Peter and Jacob with the chores."

"I don't want Leon out there with him."

"We are a part of this family now. I am Jacob's wife. You may as well get used to the idea that he is now your father."

"He is *not* my father and never will be," I muttered to myself.

"We are a family now. For better or for worse. I know it seems like it has only been for worse so far, but spring is coming. It is bound to get better. You will see. Pray and have faith."

A half hour later while I got dressed for bed, heavy footsteps on the back porch signaled the return of Uncle Jacob, Peter, and Leon from the barn. I buried myself under the quilt and turned off the flame in the kerosene lamp at my bedside. *I'll never call him Papa.*

2
FIRST DAY AT SCHOOL

I woke to warm rays of sun streaming through the bedroom window and falling onto my patchwork quilt. I'd awakened to sunlight and bird song for eight days straight now.

Mary was dressed and had brushed her long, thick, dark brown hair. She wound it into a knot before covering it dutifully with a black bonnet. She was already beautiful with finely proportioned features and high cheekbones. Her dark hair and green eyes were striking against her fair skin.

I sighed as I attempted to comb my fingers through my tangled ash brown hair, which was impossible to keep tidy.

When Mary noticed me watching her, she sneered, "What are you looking at?"

"Your hair is so pretty." I smiled. I'd made a vow two weeks ago to be nice to Mary, no matter what. So far, it hadn't made any difference.

"It's about time you woke up. Class starts in two hours," Mary replied curtly as she headed downstairs.

I get to start schul *today*. No wonder I slept in so long this morning. I was too excited to fall asleep until hours after I'd gone to bed. I hadn't been to school since coming to Virginia, and in my opinion, it was the best part of living. I longed to be a schoolteacher myself someday.

Mennonite children usually didn't attend school beyond eighth grade, so I only had two years left. The church considered any higher level of education useless and even worse – vain. Boys were expected to be farmers and girls to be wives and mothers. Nearly fifteen years old, Mary was in her last year of school. She had been adding linens to her hope chest in anticipation of her wedding for years. It was nearly full.

I had no interest in such things. All I wanted to do was teach. And a married woman was not allowed to teach.

I straightened the quilt on the bed. Mama was right about spring. The sunshine cheered everyone. Even Uncle Jacob seemed less angry.

He still shot menacing glares at times but had not lashed out at anyone since he last slapped Mary. Maybe Brother Troyer's sermon on peacemaking two Sundays back had helped. He was still cold and silent, though, and I liked it best when he was working long hours outside on the farm.

After choosing a light blue dress that matched my eyes, I tediously worked tangles out of my hair before wrapping it in a knot at the back of my head. Despite my best efforts, wayward strands fell across my forehead. After dressing, I joined Mary and my mother in the warm kitchen.

Uncle Jacob and the bigger boys were all outside tending to the cows. Magdalena had not yet woken up. Sleepy-eyed Amos emerged from the boys' room, his dark brown hair sticking up in two funny-looking tufts on each side of his head.

I giggled. "Amos, your hair is all *stroobly*. You have an extra pair of ears on your head. I'll fix it after breakfast."

"*D-Danke*," Amos stammered. Amos had developed a stutter after our papa died.

Mama thought it best to be patient, ignore it, and pray that he outgrew it. At least he was speaking again.

He pulled on his boots to go out to the chicken coop to gather eggs. He seemed so different than the cheerful little boy he'd been back in Pennsylvania. Now he was timid and solemn as if life itself was a burden.

"Susanna, the hotcakes will not make themselves." Mama broke into my thoughts to remind me to mix the batter.

Just as breakfast was ready – steaming buckwheat hotcakes with maple syrup and molasses, fragrant fried ham, and scrambled eggs – Uncle Jacob and the boys came in from the barn, stinking of cow, as usual, despite having removed the coveralls they wore when working with the livestock. We took our places around the table, and Uncle Jacob handed the big, black Bible to Leon. It was his turn to read the Scripture. Each morning Uncle Jacob chose a passage in the Bible to read before breakfast and again after supper. For the past week we had been reading the book of Daniel.

"Chapter seven," Uncle Jacob growled as Leon fumbled for the right place.

"*In the first year of Belshazzar king of Babylon Daniel had a dream and visions of his head upon his bed: then he wrote the dream, and told the sum of the matters...*" Leon read. He looked up at Uncle Jacob.

"Go on. Whole chapter."

Leon continued, "*Daniel spake and said, 'I saw in my vision by night, and, behold, the four winds of the heaven strove upon the great sea. And four great breasts'* — I mean *beasts. Beasts!*" Leon's voice rose to a squeak.

Uncle Jacob's face turned red, his eyes flashing with rage.

Mary gasped.

I smothered my giggles in an instant.

"How *darest* you mock Scripture," Uncle Jacob roared, looking alternately at Leon and me.

Leon's cheeks were bright pink, and tears collected in his eyes.

My heart pounded. I wanted to grab him and run out the door. Instead, I sat motionless, clutching my hands together to keep the trembling at bay.

"Jacob, he did not mean to – " began Mama.

"Do not contradict me, Elizabeth," seethed Uncle Jacob. "*Gott im himmel, fraa.* He should take more care when reading the Word of God."

Mama looked down, her expression angry but resigned.

Uncle Jacob was quiet a moment, all the while glaring at Leon.

The silence was stifling. I held my breath, my mind racing and my body tense.

Finally, he said evenly, "You will memorize Daniel chapter seven through verse seven when you return from school today, and you will recite it to me after supper – this in addition to your chores."

Leon stared at the floor, his brow furrowed.

I exhaled in one long breath. He wasn't going to get a beating.

I was glad when it was finally time to leave for school and I could escape the dark, oppressive house that still did not feel like home.

Mary walked at a brisk pace, obviously trying to put distance between herself and the rest of us. Peter tried his best to keep up with her.

I lagged behind with my brothers. I scowled at Mary's back. If she didn't like me, at least she could introduce me to some other girls.

The walk to school didn't take long. The dusty road was pleasant enough with its canopy of maple, elm, and dogwood trees in which birds twittered and squirrels chattered. The blue-gray Massanutten Mountains rose in the distant southeast. My excitement grew as I took in the view of the plain, wooden schoolhouse surrounded by apple trees and a grassy area in which to run and play.

Several children chased each other in the schoolyard, shouting and shrieking with laughter. A proper-looking woman appeared in the doorway, rang a brass bell, and disappeared back inside. She was tall and pretty behind gold-framed spectacles, with dark hair pulled back severely from her face.

That must be the *schul* teacher. I was nearly giddy with anticipation. I liked her already.

Upon hearing the bell, the children quickly ended their game of chase and clambered up the steps into the building, with Mary, Peter, Leon, Amos, and me right behind them.

The teacher stood at the door, greeted each child with a handshake, and asked the same question: "Will you be an obedient child today?"

"Yes, Sister Brubaker," they each replied solemnly before entering the room and filing into their seats.

After greeting her teacher and promising to be an obedient child, Mary clutched my arm and pulled me forward. "Sister Brubaker, these are my cousins, Susanna, Leon, and Amos Stutzman." She gestured toward each one of us in turn.

"I know who they are," Sister Brubaker said curtly, without looking at us. "The bishop said they were coming, although I told him I didn't think I could possibly manage even one more child, let alone three. Well, so be it. The girl will sit in the empty desk behind you, and the boys shall sit up front between Samuel and Jeb."

Bewildered, I looked through the open door at the quiet, well-behaved children waiting to begin their lessons, several empty desks among them. I felt unwanted. Why did our teacher consider my brothers and me such a huge burden?

Reaching her hand toward me, Sister Brubaker asked coldly, "Will you be an obedient child today?"

"*Ja*, Sister Brubaker," I murmured, looking at my shoes.

"Please do not mumble. It is unbecoming. Look at me when I am speaking to you," Sister Brubaker snapped.

I looked up.

"You will speak only English in this classroom."

Chagrined, I nodded.

My teacher's lips pursed in disapproval.

"Yes, Sister Brubaker."

"Well, what are you standing there for? Please take your seat."

"Yes, ma'am." Maybe I didn't like her after all. She clearly didn't like us, and I didn't know why. I slid into my seat behind Mary.

During our lunch break, I found Leon alone under an apple tree behind the school. I sat next to him. He held his Bible in his lap open to Daniel chapter seven. I peeked in his lunch pail. The food looked untouched.

I ruffled his hair. "You need to eat."

He stared at his Bible. "I need to memorize seven verses. I don't want a beating."

"You can eat while you memorize." I took a buttered roll from his lunch pail and handed it to him. "Here. When you're done eating, you can practice saying it to me."

We ate in silence. Occasionally he looked up and stared at the horizon, his lips moving in mute recitation.

Amos peeked around the corner of the building. When he saw us, he ran and threw himself into my arms, burying his head in my shoulder. Sobs shook his tiny frame. Leon looked up in alarm.

"Amos, what happened?" I asked when his sobs turned to hiccups.

"I-I want to go h-home. I-I want Mama."

I squeezed him tightly. "Are you having a hard first day?"

"T-Teacher doesn't l-like me," he stammered.

"She doesn't like any of us," Leon muttered under his breath.

"Don't pay her any mind. She's crabby today. She'll like us when she gets to know us. Especially you, Amos. Everybody likes you." I kissed him on his wet cheek. "Now let's eat something. The day will be over soon, and we'll all go home."

Leon groaned and returned his attention to the book of Daniel.

Amos climbed onto my lap and reached into his lunch pail. Leaning back against my chest, he munched on an apple.

"I'm ready," Leon said after a final swallow. He handed the Bible to me and began to recite. "Daniel seven, verses one through seven. *In the first year of Belshazzar king of Babylon Daniel had a dream of his head —* "

"*Dream* and visions *of his head*," I corrected.

"Daniel had a dream and visions of his head upon his bed: Then he wrote his dream –"

"*The* dream, not *his* dream," I interrupted again.

"*The dream*," Leon continued, "*and told the sum of it.*"

"*And told the sum of the matters.*"

The bell rang, signaling the end of lunch.

"I'll never get this memorized in time!" Leon cried, his voice cracking.

"We'll practice on the way home, too, and more once we get home. You'll get it."

Leon wiped his eyes with his sleeve. We placed our uneaten food back in our lunch pails, trudged around to the front of the building, and entered the classroom full of happy, chattering children – would we ever be one of them?

3
Provoke Not

After dinner that evening, Uncle Jacob pushed back in his chair and said, "Leon, fetch my Bible from next to my bed."

Leon quickly obeyed and stood before him.

"Turn to Daniel chapter seven."

His fingers trembling, Leon fumbled through the pages, looking for Daniel.

After a moment of waiting, Uncle Jacob held out his large, calloused hand and grumbled, "Give it here. You are slower than molasses, aren't you?" He flipped through the pages until he found it. "Begin."

Leon cleared his throat. "Daniel seven, verses one through seven. *In the first year of Belshazzar king of Babylon Daniel had a dream and visions of his head upon his bed: Then he wrote his dream —* "

"*The* dream," Uncle Jacob corrected.

"Girls, let's get the table cleared." Mama stood and picked up dirty plates. Mary and I did the same.

"*The dream and told the sum of the…of the…matters*," Leon continued. "*Daniel spake and said, 'I saw in my vision, and, behold –* "

"*I saw in my vision by night.* You forgot *by night.* Did you study this like I told you to or not?" His voice grew angry.

"I did. I tried."

"You best not be lying to me, boy."

"I'm not lying. I even studied it during lunch at school."

"Mary!" Uncle Jacob barked.

Mary's head jerked up, and her eyes widened. She turned to him. "*Ja*, Papa?"

"Did you see Leon studying his verses at lunch today?"

"I didn't see him at lunch today," Mary said sweetly. "I didn't see Susanna or Amos, either. I don't know what they were doing during lunch."

"We were behind the school. Leon studied his verses the whole time," I said.

Uncle Jacob shot an angry glare my way. "Was I speaking to you?"

"No." I lowered my head and picked up two more dirty plates, nearly dropping one in my haste. I took them to Mama. She squeezed my arm reassuringly.

"Well, go on," Uncle Jacob said to Leon. "Start over from the beginning."

Leon began again but by now was so nervous he stumbled even more than the first time.

"I don't believe you studied these at all." Uncle Jacob's eyes narrowed.

"I did. You didn't give me enough time!" Leon cried.

The heavy Bible Uncle Jacob held banged to the table as he stood, his chair protesting with an abrupt screech.

Magdalena shrieked and hid behind Mama, clutching fistfuls of Mama's skirt in her tiny hands. She released her grip when Mary picked her up. Whimpering, she buried her face in Mary's neck. Amos scampered behind as Mary carried her upstairs.

Uncle Jacob took a step toward Leon.

I had just picked up a serving dish but dropped it back on the table with a clatter. Without stopping to think, I whirled between the two of them. "You want a verse? I have a verse for you! Ephesians 6:4: *And, ye fathers, provoke not your children to wrath: but bring them up in the nurture and admonition of the Lord."*

Uncle Jacob's hand swung up, and my stomach lurched. He was going to hit me. I cringed.

A moment before the back of his hand made contact with my cheek, Mama grabbed his elbow and screamed, "No!"

I stumbled to the other side of the table.

His eyes blazed, and his face grew red and distorted. He jerked his arm away from Mama and raised it as if to slap her.

Instead of moving away from him, she wrapped her arms around his waist and pressed her cheek into his chest. "Please!"

He lowered his hand, peeled her arms away, and took a step backward, fury and confusion competing in his eyes.

Mama looked at the floor, trembling. I wanted to run to her, but I couldn't move. I couldn't even breathe.

"Do you think it right to allow your children to sass me?" Uncle Jacob snarled.

Mama kept her head bowed. "No, of course not. Please, let us not talk about this now. You and I can talk about it later tonight after the children are in bed."

"I always thought my brother was too soft. This may be how you and he raised your children, but in my house, there will be no sassing me."

Mama's face reddened. "I agree. Let us talk about the best way to discipline the children later."

"I am the man of this house, and you best be remembering your place, *fraa*. I will discipline them as I see fit."

"*Ja*, Jacob." Her voice quavered.

Uncle Jacob glared at her for a long moment, then walked to the door and grabbed his overcoat off the peg on the wall. "Peter. Leon. We have chores to do."

He stalked out. The door slammed behind him, rattling the windows and wall hangings.

Mama sank down into a chair, her head in her hands.

That's when I noticed I was shaking. I sank to the floor. Leon flung himself into my arms. Tears streamed down my cheeks as I held him.

Peter, who had been silently watching from his place at the table, stood and walked toward us. He bent down and squeezed my shoulder before joining his father outside.

Leon wiped the tears off his face and followed him.

I turned to Mama. "Do you think Leon's going to be safe out there?"

"*Ja.*" Her voice was weary. "We must finish cleaning up."

Mary came down the stairs carrying Magdalena. "Where's Papa?"

"He went to do chores. Thank you for taking care of Magdalena, Mary." Mama lifted the toddler from her arms.

I ignored Mary, angry she'd not stood up for Leon when Uncle Jacob had asked her if she'd seen him studying his verses at school. To be fair, I didn't remember seeing her at lunch, either, so it would have been a lie to say she saw him studying. I didn't care, though. I was still mad at her.

The house was unusually quiet after Uncle Jacob and the two older boys returned. I had already put Magdalena to bed and trudged outside to use the privy. When I returned to the house, Mama and Uncle Jacob were in their bedroom. As I passed it on the way to the stairs, voices murmured from behind the closed door, Mama's soft and Uncle Jacob's edgy but not as heated as before.

Peter and Leon met me at the top of the stairs. Leon's brow furrowed. "Have you seen Amos?"

"No. Isn't he in your room?"

"No. I thought maybe he went to the privy."

"I was there only a minute ago. I didn't see him."

Peter walked past me and started downstairs. "He must be outside."

"I'll help you look."

The three of us donned our coats and stepped outside where our boots waited on the back porch. While pulling them on, we called in a loud whisper, "Amos!"

No reply.

We walked around the perimeter of the house, calling more loudly. We looked behind trees and shrubbery. I peeked inside the summer kitchen. Nothing.

"What about the cellar?" Peter asked.

"Oh, I know where he is." I turned toward the back door.

"Where?"

"He's in the house. I'll show you."

They followed me inside and up the stairs.

"Wait here. Mary's in bed already," I whispered at the door to the girls' bedroom.

I tiptoed over to the chiffarobe and opened the door. Dim rays of light from the kerosene lamp on my bedside table lit the interior enough to reveal the form of a sleeping boy. "Amos," I whispered.

Gentle snores were his only reply.

I shook his arm until he woke up and blinked hard. "I-is it over?" he asked.

"*Ja*. Come. It's time to get into your own bed."

He followed me out the door, his hand in mine.

"What was he doing in there?" Peter asked.

"Hiding," Leon said, taking Amos's hand.

"What from?"

"From the devil," Leon muttered.

"Leon!" I admonished. "What a terrible thing to say."

Peter stared as Leon led Amos into the boys' bedroom. "*Ja*," he murmured, "the devil."

I shuddered. I had stood up to Uncle Jacob, and he was not likely to forget it.

4
MYSTERY IN THE DARK

I COULD NOT SLEEP. I HAD BECOME ACCUSTOMED to sleepless nights since the wagon accident, often waking from nightmares of the horrifying tumble followed by the staring eyes and broken body of my lifeless father. I hadn't had any nightmares tonight, though, because I hadn't yet fallen asleep.

My thoughts were consumed by the apology Leon and I had to give Uncle Jacob before we went to bed. Mama had insisted on it.

I stood before him, trembling. "I-I'm sorry I was disrespectful toward you. It won't happen again." I didn't mean it.

I may as well have saved my breath. He glowered at me and ordered me to clean out the chicken coop on Saturday as a punishment.

"If you ever sass me again, you will get the switch for certain," he warned.

I lowered my head and nodded.

"Do you hear me?" he shouted.

I jumped. "*Ja*, Uncle Jacob." Black hatred for him threatened to choke me. I gulped.

He had agreed to give Leon until Saturday to recite the passage from Daniel perfectly, or he would have to join me in the chicken coop.

"Don't worry. I'll help you anyway," Leon whispered to me once we got back upstairs.

My thoughts turned to the cold welcome my brothers and I had received from our teacher that morning. Why didn't she like us? Sister Brubaker wasn't outright cruel, but neither was she kind. She barely looked at us, never called on us to answer a question, and didn't speak to any of us directly unless absolutely necessary.

Sighing, I swung my legs out from under the covers and crept out of bed. The cool, wooden floorboards felt good on my hot feet as I tiptoed to the window. As had become my habit on these restless nights, I gazed out the window at our garden to the north and the chicken coop beyond it on our side of the weathered wooden fence. The grapevines along the fence line appeared silvery in the moonlight. On the other side stood the home and barn of our neighbor.

I spied a lantern hung in the barn loft's window. That was curious.

I did not know much about this neighbor except that she was an older woman named Lydia Swartzendruber, who lived with her feeble-minded brother, Skip. They were at church every Sunday. Church members rarely spoke of her, but when they did, they referred to her as Aunt Lydia, as was customary with older, unmarried women in the church. She sat alone on the women's side during the service and left right afterward. I had noticed church members nod politely when passing her, but I had never seen anyone speak with her. Uncle Jacob said she rented out fields her father had owned on the other side of town. He'd also given us children a strict command to never set a foot upon her property.

When I asked why, he thundered, "Do you need a reason to follow my orders? Never you mind why. Only see that you obey."

Later, Peter told Leon and me that the mysterious neighbor was a witch. "If she catches you looking at her, she'll turn herself into a bird and peck out your eyes at night."

I didn't really believe Peter, but remembering his words, I shuddered at the image and squeezed my eyes shut as if protecting them from a menacing bird.

When I opened my eyes, I looked out the window again, hoping to catch a glimpse of the doe I'd spied the week before. Instead, illuminated by a nearly-full moon, a wagon crept up the lane to my neighbor's barn. It appeared to be loaded with straw.

The shadowy figure of a man climbed off the wagon seat and opened the barn door. After driving the wagon into the barn, he strode to the back of the house. A few minutes later, he returned to the barn carrying a large basket. The figure of a woman followed him. I could tell it was Aunt Lydia by her shape and the way she walked.

I watched the barn for what seemed a long time. What were they doing in there? It must have been something quite wicked if they were skulking about in the dark. No wonder Uncle Jacob would not have us associating with such people.

Finally, both figures emerged from the barn. Aunt Lydia walked toward the house, and the man drove away in a now-empty wagon.

They must have been unloading the straw. But why take a delivery in the middle of the night?

Perhaps the straw hid something else. Something Aunt Lydia could get in trouble for. Something bad. Now I had a new mystery to puzzle over, but it would have to wait until morning. Yawning, I returned to bed, unable to keep my eyes open any longer.

The mood at breakfast was chillier than usual. After Mary's flawless reading of Daniel chapter eight, the family – each member consumed with his or her own thoughts – ate the breakfast of bacon, fried eggs, and grits in silence.

Wishing to ease the stifling tension, I said, "I saw something that wondered me last night."

"And what would that be?" asked Mama with a tired smile. Her face was pale.

"In the middle of the night, a wagon filled with straw drove into Aunt Lydia's barn and came out empty." I decided it best not to mention Aunt Lydia had entered the barn with a man.

"I will not have you spying on the neighbors," snapped Uncle Jacob.

"I was not spying. I could not sleep. I…"

Mama shot me a warning glance.

"Do not talk back to me," he ordered, the quietness of his voice even more menacing than when he shouted. "You are never to go there. Mind your own business. Whatever goes on over there has nothing to do with you. Do you understand me?"

"*Ja*, Uncle Jacob," I whispered, resigning myself to unanswered questions and a silent breakfast.

5
A NEW FRIEND

MAMA HUGGED US GOOD-BYE AT THE DOOR AS WE left for school. All except for Mary, who bristled whenever Mama touched her. She hadn't been that way when we first moved to Virginia. She was warm and affectionate to all of us until Uncle Jacob and Mama married. Peter only allowed Mama to hug him when Mary wasn't around. He stiffened and pulled away if Mary was in the room.

This morning Mary was still upstairs as Mama wrapped Peter in her arms. He had been starved for a mother's affection his whole life and relished it now, melting into her embrace. When Mary came downstairs, however, he abruptly pulled away, guilt flashing across his face. Mary scowled.

I was relieved to escape to school. I decided for now, Sister Brubaker's cold demeanor toward my brothers and me was more tolerable than Uncle Jacob's bad temper. I tried my best to be respectful, polite, and studious while stifling my growing disappointment as Sister Brubaker ignored my efforts.

She met my friendly greeting that morning with a silent nod followed by her customary request for obedience. This would not be hurtful in itself, but when I watched Sister Brubaker greet the other girls my age much more warmly, an ache lodged in my heart.

During our grammar lesson, a subject in which I felt confident, I raised my hand almost every time Sister Brubaker asked a question, but she did not acknowledge me, except once when no one else volunteered.

When we took a break for lunch, I sat outside alone on the front steps with my lunch pail and watched Leon play tag with five other boys. Amos knelt under a maple tree with a quiet, gentle boy named Paul who had befriended him. They appeared to be examining a bug crawling in the dirt. It was good to see my brothers laughing and making friends.

Mary sat with two of the older girls under an apple tree across the schoolyard. After Mary said something to them, they laughed and glanced at me. When they saw I was watching, they quickly looked away.

My cheeks burned.

"May I sit here?"

I looked up to see Martha, a girl my age, smiling at me. She had dimples and slightly crooked teeth. Her bonnet hung by its strings down her back, exposing fine, blond hair.

"*Ja*, of course." I quickly scooted over and patted the step next to me.

"My mama told me you used to live in Harrisonburg when you were little," she said.

"I did. We moved to Pennsylvania when I was four because Papa wanted his own farm."

"Why did you move back?"

"After Grandpa died, a chimney fire burned down Grandma Clara's house, and she moved into town with Aunt Ann," I began.

"I remember that fire." Martha reached into her lunch pail and pulled out a hunk of cornbread.

"Last summer the railroad in Pennsylvania bought Papa's land, so he decided the time was right to move back to Virginia and take over my grandpa's farm."

Martha frowned. "I'm sorry about your papa."

"*Danke*." I didn't know what else to say.

Martha lifted the dish towel covering her pail. "I brought you something," she said with a smile. "I wanted to welcome you properly." She pulled out a piece of red-striped hard candy. "It's leftover *tzooker* from Christmas, but it should still be good. I want you to have it."

"Oh, Martha...*danke*," I exclaimed. "That is the nicest thing anyone has done for me since I came to Virginia. I wish I had something for you."

"Well, I want you to feel welcome here at school. Sister Brubaker doesn't seem to be doing a very good job of that."

"You noticed, did you?"

"Please don't fret about it." Martha's voice lowered to nearly a whisper. "Sister Brubaker is usually really nice. She's cross because Brother Jacob married your mother instead of her. They used to be sweethearts, you know."

My eyes grew round. "How do you know that?"

"Everybody knows it. People often saw them talking together after church on Sundays. We thought they seemed sweet on each other and would marry. Then it stopped. I don't know why. She must have held out hope, though, until Brother Jacob married your mother. Now she'll probably never marry. That's why she acts angry at you and your brothers."

"But we had nothing to do with it. It was Grandma Clara and Great Aunt Ann's idea Mama and Uncle Jacob should marry each other. Grandma Clara's house was too small for all of us, and the noise got on Aunt Ann's nerves. It made her *grexy* all the time. They thought Uncle Jacob needed a wife, so they talked to the church elders about it. They agreed and called the bishop in to persuade Uncle Jacob and Mama to get married."

I still remembered the bishop's words to Mama as they sat in Grandma Clara and Aunt Ann's parlor: *The Lord would not have you be a burden on the church, Elizabeth. Grieving over John will not bring him back. It is only false pride that keeps you from embracing this God-given opportunity to share a home with a worthy man.*

"My brothers and I had nothing to do with it," I repeated.

"It doesn't matter. You remind her of what she's lost. She was this way with Mary and Peter at first, too, but she's better to them now. She'll get over it, I suspect. Then she'll be nice to you, too." Martha took a bite of cornbread.

I reached into my pail and pulled out a slightly bruised apple. "I don't have anything as good as *tzooker*," I said, "but would you like this?"

Martha giggled. "I already have one. Say we are friends, and we're even."

"We're friends." I smiled widely, mirroring Martha's expression.

That night, sleep eluded me again as I thought about Uncle Jacob's prior courtship with Sister Brubaker. Reliving my moments on the steps with Martha, I smiled in the darkness. It felt good to have a new friend. Surrounded always by family, I hadn't realized how lonely I'd been.

Through the slightly open window, the sound of a dog barking in the distance interrupted my thoughts. I scooted out of bed and tiptoed to the window, not wanting to wake Mary. I pulled the curtains apart.

No mysterious lanterns or wagons tonight. The moonlight dusted the treetops with silver. An owl hooted nearby. A cat crouched in the grass, prepared to pounce on its unsuspecting midnight feast. Subtle movement in the shadows caught my eyes. The doe had returned, along with another. They grazed peacefully under a crabapple tree near the fence.

Suddenly, their heads jerked upright, and they stared briefly in the same direction before leaping into the darkness.

I craned my neck to see what startled them but quickly stepped backward. Aunt Lydia had left her house and was heading toward the barn. This time no man accompanied her, but she carried a heavy-looking basket in her arms. She was in the barn no more than a minute before she emerged again and walked toward the house, her arms empty. Why had she left the basket in the barn? What was in it?

I leaned toward the windowpane again, trying to get a better look. She stopped and glanced up toward me. My heart skipped a beat and began to race. I fell back into the shadows. Had she seen me? I waited a moment until the beats in my chest returned to almost normal, then crouched down and peeked through the outside edge of the curtain. She was nowhere in sight.

What was she hiding in that barn? Stolen property? Moonshine? The desire to sneak over there and snoop was almost overwhelming, but if I were caught, my uncle's wrath would be severe. No, I had better not risk that. A gust of cool air blew through the window, raising goose bumps on my arms. I pulled it shut, closed the curtains, and crawled into bed.

6
WHO'S TO BLAME?

THE STENCH OF CHICKEN DROPPINGS ASSAULTED my nostrils as I picked through the straw, looking for eggs. It had been a few weeks since I'd been ordered to clean the coop, but I still caught a faint whiff of vinegar that I had used to scrub the roosts and nesting boxes.

Chickens clucked and squawked indignantly as though I were stealing from them. I supposed I was. Through the din the boys' laughter rang outside the coop along with the familiar *whump* as a bat made contact with a stiff canvas ball. The boys were taking full advantage of the unusually warm April night.

We had brought baseball with us to Virginia, and Peter was enthralled, as Papa had been. Papa had first heard men talking about the New York

Knickerbockers when he went to a hog auction in town and later read accounts of the games in the newspaper. He had carved a bat and enlisted Mama to sew a ball packed with straw. Back home in Pennsylvania, Papa, Leon, Amos, and I played until the sun went down on long summer evenings after chores were finished. Afraid the church would frown upon this worldly new activity, it had been our family's secret.

I stepped out into the chicken yard with a full basket of eggs, squinting in the glare of the sun as it began to set in the west. Leon held the bat against his shoulder, waiting for Peter to pitch the ball. Amos stood behind Leon, poised to catch it if he missed.

"C-come on, Leon!" Amos yelled. "Y-you can do it!"

Leon had a big grin on his face. "Sure, I can do it – that is, *if* Peter ever learns to throw right," he teased.

"How's *this* throw?" Peter asked, hurling the ball directly at Leon's groin. Leon leapt out of the way just in time, and all three boys howled with laughter. Uncle Jacob stood near the barn, watching with interest as the boys played. He shifted his eyes and caught me looking at him. His features twisted into a familiar scowl, and he turned to enter the barn.

The corner of my mouth turned up in a wry smile. Papa and the boys weren't the only Stutzman men intrigued with baseball.

I lifted the latch on the gate and stepped out, carefully closing the gate behind me. As I turned to make sure it was latched, I heard another *whump* as the bat made contact. The ball sailed over my head and into the chicken yard with a thud. Peter, taking his turn as catcher, ran past me after the ball. As I headed toward the house, I called over my shoulder, "Don't forget to latch it."

"Susanna, is that you?" Mama called from the parlor when I stepped into the kitchen.

"*Ja*, Mama."

"Magdalena is in her crib. She wants you to sing to her."

I set the egg basket on the floor next to the cellar door and washed my hands in the basin Mama had prepared for me.

Magdalena stood in her crib, clutching the sides to hold herself up. "'Sanna," she sang out when I walked in. She hopped up and down in celebration. Letting go of the sides, she reached her arms toward me and fell backward on her rear.

I laughed. "Silly girl. Lie down now, and I'll sing you a song."

Magdalena grinned and plopped onto her side, ready for her bedtime ritual. I covered her with a blanket, sat in the rocker next to the crib, and sang while rubbing her back.

Halfway through the first verse of the hymn, the back kitchen door slammed, and snatches of the boys' banter and laughter floated through the bedroom wall. Mama shushed them.

I finished the first verse and looked at Magdalena. She stared at me with wide eyes. I began the second verse.

The back door opened again. "Susanna!" bellowed Uncle Jacob.

My heart leapt into my throat. *What have I done?*

I strode toward the bedroom door and opened it, knowing better than to make him wait. Magdalena whimpered.

"I'm here. What is it?" I asked, stepping into the kitchen and closing the door behind me.

Mary, eager to see me reprimanded, peeked her head around the corner to gawk from the stairwell.

Magdalena's whimpers turned into wailing.

"The chickens are running loose all over," Uncle Jacob snarled. "You forgot to latch the gate to the chicken yard."

Mary smirked and walked past me into the bedroom to comfort Magdalena. She shut the door behind her.

Did I? I tried to remember. An image entered my mind of the ball flying over my head into the chicken yard.

I glanced at Peter. He stared at me, the color draining from his face.

"I'm sorry. I'll catch them," I said, heading toward the back door.

"Oh, Susanna," Mama said, disappointed.

"Papa, it was my fault," Peter blurted. "The ball went in there. I forgot to latch the gate when I fetched it."

I stopped and turned back to look at Uncle Jacob.

He glared at Peter. "Get the switch," he growled.

Peter turned to obey. Leon and Amos looked on with sympathy.

"No!" I blurted.

They all looked at me, shocked at my outburst.

"Peter is not to blame. I am," I said. "Sh-shall I get the switch?"

"But I – " Peter began.

"It was my fault. I-I was the last one in the coop," I said firmly. It wasn't really a lie. Peter may have been the last one in the chicken yard, but I *had* been the last one in the coop itself. I hoped my half-lie would convince Uncle Jacob to blame me.

Uncle Jacob's gaze shifted between us, anger and confusion twisting his expression into a scowl.

Peter stared at me, his mouth open. Amos and Leon looked similarly stunned.

"Shall I get the switch?" I asked again, my voice trembling.

"Jacob," Mama said softly, touching his arm.

He shot a warning glance at her with narrowed eyes, his face tense.

"I suggest you have her go out and catch those chickens. She will remember that lesson longer than a swat from a switch." Her voice sounded strained as she forced a stern tone. When she turned to look at me, sympathy registered in her eyes just before they flickered and she stumbled forward.

"Mama!" I shrieked, running to her, Leon right behind me.

Uncle Jacob grabbed her before she fell and helped her into a chair. He brushed her hair back from her ashen face. "Elizabeth, you need to lie down."

"Mama, you nearly fainted!" I cried, grabbing her hands.

"I am fine. I have not been feeling well. Jacob is right. I think I need to lie down." She tried to stand.

Uncle Jacob and Leon helped her to the bedroom.

Mary was sitting in the rocker next to Magdalena's crib. Her eyes widened when she saw Mama. "What happened?"

"She has taken ill. That is all," Uncle Jacob explained.

I stood outside the door and watched them help her into bed and tuck the covers around her, his sudden tenderness in sharp contrast to the fury he displayed only moments before. Amos and Peter stood behind me.

Magdalena stood and held her arms out. "Mama!"

Mary helped her lie back down and murmured to her in soothing tones.

"Should we fetch Grandma Clara?" I asked.

Mama smiled. "I am fine. Truly I am. Just a touch of a stomach ailment. You go catch those chickens now."

Uncle Jacob turned back to me, his tone stern again. "Do not come in until you have caught them all."

I fled out the door, relieved I didn't have to experience the switch. Not yet, anyway. Who knows what may have happened if Mama had not taken ill? I shuddered. I had never experienced a beating before. Still, I worried for Mama, and catching chickens was no fun. I hoped I wouldn't be out there all night.

The chickens bunched together in one corner of the side yard, foraging near the garden. The rooster cackled and strutted as I approached. I stopped and sprinkled some sunflower seeds on the ground. The chickens clucked and moved toward me. I crept up slowly behind the rooster. I had to grab him first. The hens would be easier to catch with him in the coop. They might even follow willingly. As I bent toward him, he ran away, squawking and flapping. The hens scattered, alarmed. This wasn't going to be easy.

Finally, after six attempts, I managed to grab the rooster on both sides, pinning his wings to his body. I held him between my arm and my chest, holding his feet together with my other hand as I carried him to the coop. I wiped the sweat from my brow and returned to the hens now clustered together. One by one, I managed to catch nearly all of them as the sun sank deeper and deeper on the horizon.

Two of them hopped the fence into the neighboring yard. I groaned. I didn't know what to do. I'd be punished if I didn't catch them, but Uncle Jacob had strictly forbidden all of us from going on Lydia Swartzendruber's property.

It was nearly dark now. No one was in sight. Weighing my options, I decided to risk getting caught on the wrong side of the fence. After all, he had ordered me to catch every one of them. I scrambled over the fence before I could change my mind.

The chickens were by the woodshed at the back of the neighbor's house. As I approached, their clucking increased in volume.

"Shush now," I said, creeping slowly behind one of them.

"Do you need some help?"

I whirled around, stifling a startled yelp. Lydia Swartzendruber, the woman Peter claimed was a witch, stood watching me. A shudder ran through me. I wanted to run, but my feet seemed staked to the ground.

"I-I'm sorry. I-I shouldn't be bothering you," I stammered. "The chickens got loose."

"No bother." She smiled. "I will corner them next to the woodpile. It will be easier to get them that way."

She was right. I easily trapped one in my arms. Before I knew it, she had the other. She waited by the fence while I took the first chicken to the coop and then came back for the one she held.

"*Danke*," I whispered.

"You are welcome." She turned and walked back to her house.

One hen was still missing. I spent another half hour looking for it, but I found no trace. Maybe a chicken hawk had already swooped down and snatched it for supper. I hoped Uncle Jacob wouldn't notice its absence.

Light glowed from the parlor when I entered the kitchen through the back door. I peeked in. Uncle Jacob was in a cushioned chair reading his Bible. His back was to me.

After washing up, I tiptoed to the bedroom where Mama slept peacefully. I studied her face and her arms looking for bruises. Although I had never witnessed Uncle Jacob striking her, I worried about it nonetheless. Why had she nearly fainted? Was she truly ill like she said?

Exhausted, I trudged to my room, changed into my nightgown, and flopped into bed next to Mary.

"Peter told me what you did," Mary said in the darkness.

I didn't respond.

"You didn't have to do that, you know. Peter can take care of himself. Mind your own business if you know what's good for you."

"Would you have rather seen him beaten again?"

"If he deserved it, *ja. He that spareth his rod hateth his son*," she said, quoting Proverbs.

"*Blessed are the merciful, for they shall obtain mercy*," I retorted with one of the Beatitudes. "I think he is too hard on Peter," I whispered before she could come up with another scripture verse. "And on you, too."

She remained mute in the darkness next to me.

I closed my eyes and rolled over onto my side with my back to her. Minutes passed. I began to drift off.

Her quiet sniffles betrayed her. She was crying.

I pretended to be asleep.

7
AUNT LYDIA

I HAD BEEN ANTICIPATING THIS SUNDAY FOR weeks: My congregation was holding a communion ceremony for the first time since I'd arrived in Virginia, and I was finally allowed to take part. Two weeks before our move to Virginia, I had been baptized, so now I joined the grownups in this solemn ceremony rather than merely watching. I sat in the back row of the women's side in the meetinghouse with Martha, Mary, and a few other older girls. Mary distanced herself from me as much as she could, but it didn't matter to me. I'd rather sit next to Martha, anyway.

When we arrived, Aunt Lydia was already sitting in the pew in front of us, alone as always. The women filed one by one into all the other rows, avoiding the one where Aunt Lydia sat, although a couple of the pews seemed crowded. It would have been funny if it weren't so unsettling.

Sitting in the front row on the men's side, Brother Engle, lead chorister, began the first hymn. He sang one line at a time, and the congregation repeated it in vigorous four-part harmony. Although the soprano line was a little high for me, I never got the knack of singing the alto harmonies. I settled for silently mouthing the highest notes in the melody. During the second hymn, Brother Troyer entered and settled behind the pulpit. With four and sometimes five verses in many of the hymns, nearly ten minutes passed before the song's conclusion.

After the hymns, we lowered ourselves to the floor, turned around, and knelt at our pews for the opening prayer. It was always in German, as was most of the sermon to follow.

When I thought my knees couldn't take the hard floor anymore, the prayer ended, and we returned to our seats. Although I understood German well, I found myself drifting in my thoughts as Brother Troyer delivered the sermon. I stifled a yawn and turned my gaze to Aunt Lydia.

She looked straight ahead, her expression serene, at least from what I saw in her profile. Why did the others avoid her? She certainly looked harmless enough, and she was kind to help me catch those two hens last month. She was plump and wore silver wire-rimmed glasses. She appeared to be in her late sixties, her dark hair streaked with silver, her bun covered with a white mesh prayer cap. A large, heavy Bible rested open in her lap, its black leather cover worn and its pages dog-eared with much use.

Brother Troyer stepped down from the pulpit, and I shifted my attention back to him. It was time for communion. A table in front of the pulpit held a large loaf of bread and a silver cup of grape juice. Brother Troyer raised the loaf with both hands and blessed it. Then, in English, he quoted from Matthew twenty-six. *"And as they were eating, Jesus took bread, and blessed it, and brake it, and gave it to the disciples, and said, 'Take, eat; this is my body."*

After tearing off a piece of bread for himself, Brother Troyer tore pieces for the elders, deacons, and choristers in the front row and proceeded to pass the loaf among all the men before coming to the women's side. I watched as the loaf diminished in size until he came to Aunt Lydia. He paused for a moment.

She met his gaze.

All eyes were on the pair now. It seemed as though the whole church held its breath in that long moment. Communion was not to be taken by a member who had unresolved conflict with another in the congregation.

Brother Troyer continued walking past the pew in which Aunt Lydia sat, his lips pressed together in a grim line.

Aunt Lydia stared straight ahead. Only the pink in her neck, creeping up to her cheeks, betrayed her hurt – or shame.

I hardly noticed when the bread was handed to me. It was dry and chewy, difficult to swallow.

Brother Troyer returned to the front, and the ritual of the blessing and Scripture reading continued with the cup of grape juice. "*And he took the cup, and gave thanks, and gave it to them, saying, 'Drink ye all of it; For this is my blood of the new testament, which is shed for many for the remission of sins.*" The cup was passed. Again, he skipped Aunt Lydia.

When the service was over, it was time for the great feast. Long tables had been set on the meetinghouse grounds. Still, we had to eat in shifts, as there was not enough space for everyone all at once. The boys and some of the younger girls sat on the ground. Martha and I chose to eat in the second shift. While waiting, we sat in the shade of an elm. It was a warm May afternoon. Cheerful lilacs bloomed in bunches along the outside wall of the church. Bees buzzed lazily for nectar. Martha picked tiny daisies dotting the grass around us, weaving them into a chain.

Aunt Lydia found Skip, and the two of them rode away together in their wagon. They weren't staying for Sunday dinner. I wondered if they would return for the foot-washing service to follow.

"Martha, I'm curious about something," I said. "Why does no one talk to Aunt Lydia?"

She continued working on the daisy chain as though she hadn't heard me.

"Martha?"

"I want to tell you, Susanna, really. But Mother and Father told me never to speak of it," she finally answered.

"It seems as though I'm the only person over the age of twelve who doesn't know."

"Then you're fortunate. I wish I didn't."

"If she's done something wicked, then why has the church not excommunicated her?" I asked. "At my church in Pennsylvania, a man divorced his wife, and he was excommunicated until he repented."

"And did he?"

"No. We did not see him again."

"I think it's best if you ask your uncle or your mother about Aunt Lydia."

"Uncle Jacob won't talk about it. He only said not to go on her property. Peter says she's a witch."

"She is not a witch. That's silly talk."

"Did she do something terribly wicked?"

Martha hesitated. "No. She only disobeyed the church's counsel."

"Is that why Brother Troyer skipped her during communion?"

"*Ja.* I think so."

"I saw her do something odd last week. I couldn't sleep, so I looked out the window and saw her outside…with a man. Does that have anything to do with – ?"

Martha clapped her hands over her ears and scrambled to stand. "I don't want to hear any more. Susanna, please don't ask any more questions of me. I've told you too much already."

"You've told me nothing," I replied, sharper than I'd meant to.

Martha looked stricken, her cheeks red.

My heart twinged with remorse. "Please forgive me. I won't ask any more questions."

She knelt and hugged me. "I forgive you. You're curious. I understand. But I need to obey my parents."

Later, after stuffing ourselves with roast chicken, mashed potatoes, sauerkraut, dinner rolls, pickles of all kinds, and berry pie, we returned to the meetinghouse. Aunt Lydia had not returned.

The last pew on each side had been moved to the wall, perpendicular now to the others. Basins of water sat on the floor in front of them with a stack of towels for each basin on the pew itself.

We filed into the pews facing the front, and Brother Showalter led us in a hymn. Next, Brother Troyer read from John thirteen describing the Passover supper when Jesus washed his disciples' feet, ending with, *"If I then, your Lord and Master, have washed your feet; ye also ought to wash one another's feet. For I have given you an example, that ye should do as I have done to you."*

When he finished, the women in the first two rows entered the anteroom to remove their shoes and stockings. The men removed theirs while sitting in their pews. Once their feet were bare, the church members walked to the basins, men on their side, women on the other. The women moved in pairs, one sitting in the pew, and the other squatting before a basin, facing her partner. Even though I'd observed this ritual twice a year for my whole life, I'd never participated. This time I watched them carefully so I knew exactly what to do when it was my turn.

After removing our shoes and stockings in the anteroom, Martha and I paired up. Martha sat and held her foot over the basin of water. Squatting in front of her, I draped the towel across my lap and reached into the basin, raising palms full of water to pour over her hovering foot. After rinsing each foot, I took it in my lap and dried it with the towel. We switched places, and Martha poured the tepid water over each of my feet in turn. With moist eyes, we embraced and kissed each other on the cheeks when we were finished. My heart stirred with tenderness toward my friend. The ritual, meant to remind us to be humble servants of others, had served its purpose well. I never wanted to hurt her again.

Still, my questions about Aunt Lydia lingered. If anything, I was even more curious now than I was before.

8
WHEN SPARROWS FALL

"HERE IS THE LAST OF IT." GRANDMA CLARA GASPED and dropped the heavy basket of dirty laundry at my feet.

Three weeks ago school had let out for summer vacation. Since then I had helped my grandmother and my great aunt Ann with household chores every Saturday. I liked this arrangement. I liked their tidy little house on the bank of Blacks Run, a stream that ran right through the middle of town. I liked Grandma Clara's undivided attention and hearing stories about when my father had been little. I liked the quiet without my younger brothers and sister around. And I liked being away from Uncle Jacob most of all.

"Grandma, may I ask you something?" My voice was tentative as I loaded the wash boiler with dingy white undergarments, food-splattered aprons, and smudged shirtwaists. Great Aunt Ann was outside in the garden, and I found it easier to talk to my grandmother when we were alone.

"Of course." She sat heavily in a nearby chair and wiped her brow with the hem of her apron. Wisps of damp, white hair had escaped from the bun at the back of her head, and she tucked them into place.

"Has Uncle Jacob always been so…strict?" I glanced at my grandmother to see whether I had overstepped good manners by asking.

Grandma Clara looked at the floor. A ripple of concern crossed her face, but she didn't immediately answer.

Nervously, I poked the soiled clothing under the water with a wash stick and placed the heavy lid on top of the boiler.

Finally, she sighed and looked at me. "Has he been harsh?"

"Well, *ja*. At least, he is not like my papa was." My face crumpled as long-held tears escaped down my cheeks, much against my will.

"Oh, my dear *kinskind*." Grandma Clara stood and wrapped her plump, warm arms around my shoulders and held me tight. "You must miss him so. I do, too."

My silent tears turned to sobs, my face red and hot. My grandmother held me close until my sobbing turned into ragged sniffles, relief flooding through me.

"I was afraid Jacob's anger would get the best of him." Grandma Clara led me to a chair at the kitchen table. "Has he hurt you?"

"No, he's only scared me, but he has whipped Peter several times, and for things I don't think he deserved whipping for." I wiped my face with the embroidered handkerchief my grandmother handed me.

"In my way of thinking, no one deserves whipping, Susanna. This grieves me. But I will answer your question. No, Jacob has not always been so…strict…as you put it. He changed when your aunt Rachel died. I hoped marrying your mother would soften him again."

"It doesn't seem to have worked." My voice cracked, and tears threatened once again. "Do you think he will hurt Mama? I fear it. She has not been well."

"We need to pray about your fears."

"That's what Mama always says" – I scoffed – "but it doesn't do any good. I don't think God even listens. Or maybe he doesn't care."

"Oh, Susanna, I know this is hard to believe, but God does care, and he does listen. Did you know he counts the number of hairs on your head?"

I sniffed defiantly, looking at the floor, ashamed for doubting God while at the same time relieved for having confessed it.

"Those are Jesus's very words. He also said God sees each sparrow that falls. It does not say sparrows won't fall, but when they do, he sees it happen. If he knows when a sparrow falls, surely he knows when bad things happen to his people."

"Well, so he knows…but he doesn't seem to *care*," I said, my eyes pleading with her to help me make some sense out of my father's death and its aftermath.

"This is where faith comes in. When terrible things happen to us – or even daily irritants of life – we have a choice of how to respond. Do we respond in faith that God loves us and will help all things to work for good, or do we respond in anger and bitterness?"

I dropped my gaze to the floor, twisting the handkerchief fretfully.

"Jacob has chosen the latter. He blames God and others for Rachel's death. Do you want to be an angry person like he is? Or do you want to choose to believe in God's love for you, despite the trials you face?"

"I don't want to be like Uncle Jacob," I admitted. "But I don't know how to stop being angry."

"The only way is to keep praying and looking for God's goodness. Look for it in the kindness of others. You do not need to be afraid to tell God how you feel. He knows already, and he is big enough to handle your anger."

"I'll try, Grandma."

Grandma Clara smiled and patted my damp cheeks. "God will be faithful, Susanna. You will see."

We sat in silence for a moment. Something my grandmother had said earlier flickered in the back of my mind. I replayed the conversation in my head until I remembered.

"Grandma, you said Uncle Jacob blamed others – besides God. What do you mean? Didn't Aunt Rachel die of milk fever after giving birth to Peter?"

"*Ja*, that's right."

"So, who would he have to blame?"

"Well, you said he was most harsh to Peter. I do think in some ways he blames Peter."

"But Peter was only a baby."

"Grief plays tricks with your mind. Anger is often a part of grief, and anger always tries to find something to land on. I think maybe part of Jacob's anger has landed on Peter because it was Peter's birth that led to Rachel's sickness."

"You said 'others.' Who else does he blame?"

"Well, Lydia Swartzendruber would be the other one."

"You mean our neighbor? Why her?"

"Because she was the midwife who delivered Peter, and because she failed to save Rachel. She did everything she knew to do, of course, but Rachel still died."

"So that's why Uncle Jacob won't let us go near her property."

Grandma Clara opened her mouth to speak but shut it again as if holding something back.

"Is that why the church members don't talk to her? Do they blame her, too?"

"Oh, no. That has nothing to do with it."

"Then why – ?"

Footsteps sounded on the porch. Great Aunt Ann had returned to the house.

"Goodness, we'd better look busy, or Ann will scold us for dawdling," Grandma Clara said with a wink. She stood with surprising swiftness for her size and moved toward the flour barrel to begin making bread.

Giggling, I picked up the wash stick and stirred the laundry in the boiler. Once again, my questions remained unanswered.

Walking home later that afternoon, I took Grandma Clara's advice and prayed like I'd never prayed before. I expressed all my anger and sorrow until I had nothing left to say. I prayed for Mama, asked God for his help, and told him I chose to trust him. Afterward, I felt lighter than I had since the accident on the way to Virginia.

When I opened the front door to my house, however, I was greeted by the strained faces of Mama and Mary.

"Susanna, I have something important to tell you," Mama said as Magdalena whimpered and clung to her neck.

9
A Day of Surprises

My chest tightened. What now? Bracing myself against a sense of something gone horribly wrong, I looked from Mama to Mary, waiting for one of them to tell me what had upset them.

Mary glowered through red-rimmed eyes, and she sniffed back tears before abruptly retreating to our shared bedroom upstairs.

"Mama, what is it?" I asked. My heart pounded. Had Uncle Jacob hurt her?

Mama set Magdalena in her high chair and handed her a biscuit. The toddler stopped whimpering and giggled with delight as she brought the biscuit to her mouth.

Mama took my hands in hers. "I am going to have another baby."

The tight feeling in my chest dropped to my stomach as if I'd been punched. Another baby! With Uncle Jacob? I jerked my hands away from Mama's and gasped. "What?"

"Oh, Susanna, please do not be upset. I understand why you are, but I simply cannot endure another young girl's angry words right now." Mama looked weary, her face pale.

Forcing myself to be calm, I sat in a chair at the table next to Magdalena's high chair.

"Eat?" Magdalena offered her biscuit to me, thrusting the soggy mass toward my face.

"No, *danke*, Maggie. You eat it." I waved my sister's hand away. I sighed, afraid to look at Mama, lest my eyes betray my confusion of feelings – anger, grief, surprise, revulsion, and yes, I admitted to myself grudgingly, a little bit of delight.

"I wanted to tell you and Mary at the same time, but she overheard Jacob and me talking about it this morning."

"Is she terribly upset?"

"It seems so," Mama replied. "I think she was holding out hope that we'd all go home – I mean return to Pennsylvania – but this makes her realize we are here to stay."

"Here to stay," I muttered. "I'm surprised, Mama. I thought you loved Papa."

"I did – I mean I still do. I *always* will." A lone tear trickled down her cheek. She brushed it away with the back of her hand. "But now I choose to love Jacob."

My head jerked up. I looked at my mother in shock. "*Love* him? How can you love him?"

"Let me explain something to you. Love is not a feeling. It is a choice to place another person in the highest regard and to want the best for him or her. It means treating someone with dignity, respect, and forgiveness, in spite of how he treats you."

"But he's so mean, Mama. Would you have married him if you had known what he was really like?"

"You know I was given no choice in the matter. If it had been up to me, and had I known of his temper…but there is no use pondering that now." She pressed her lips together, resignation on her face. "I do not like how he punishes Mary and Peter, or even the rest of you, for that matter. At least he has not struck you or your sister or brothers. I do believe we would return home to Pennsylvania if he were to do that."

My heart leapt, fear striking against hope from hearing my mother say *return home*. "But where would we go? Our house is gone. That land doesn't belong to us anymore."

She sighed. "I confess I do not know. Perhaps someone in the church would take us in until I found work. I can sew. I can clean houses." She shook her head. "I should not even talk this way."

"I can work also. I don't have to finish school." I gulped.

"There will be no need for that. Things will get better. There is goodness in him yet."

"How can you believe that?"

She sat in a chair next to me. "Do you remember Jacob at all before Rachel died?"

"Not really."

"He was a good man once. Rachel and I were schoolmates and friends. She married Jacob, and two years later I married your father. We spent many happy evenings visiting together in this very house before moving to Pennsylvania. Rachel became my closest friend, and Jacob was like a dear brother. He was very funny and clever with his hands. When you were two and Mary was three, he made each of you a tiny doll cradle for Christmas. Do you remember that?"

"That was Uncle Jacob?" A distant memory fluttered through my mind like a trapped butterfly. There was a bearded man who joked and laughed and gave me sweets. I remembered that Christmas when the man gave me the small wooden cradle with stars carved into the sides. "That was Uncle Jacob?" I repeated, incredulously.

"*Ja*. And I believe he still is like that, but he has lost his way. Sometimes when we are alone I get a glimpse of him like he used to be, and those moments make it easier for me to choose to love him."

"If only he had more such moments," I muttered.

"I agree. I only ask for your courage and patience. And promise me you will marry a gentle, kind man – one who loves you as much as I do."

"I promise, but I don't think I want to be married." I could not imagine it. I had never told anyone, not even Mama, of my longing to be a teacher.

Mama smiled. "I expect you will change your mind when you are older."

I took a deep breath and forced a smile, determined to be happy for my mother's sake. "So when will I meet my new sister or brother?" I asked.

"In five months – November." Mama rubbed her belly.

I was surprised I hadn't noticed its growing roundness. It did seem her "stomach ailment" had lasted longer than usual. Now I understood why. "When will you tell the boys?"

"Probably in another month. I will not be able to hide it much longer."

"Is Uncle Jacob happy?"

"He says he is, but I believe it brings back sad memories and makes him worry. Maybe that is not such a bad thing. He seems to be making a greater effort to control his temper so as not to upset me."

My mother was right. Uncle Jacob had been more patient. When Leon had broken a tree limb by hanging on it, I expected Uncle Jacob to yell, but he had only spoken gruffly about being careful to choose sturdier limbs.

"Aunt Elizabeth." Mary stood uncertainly at the bottom of the stairs.

"Mary, I did not realize you were there," Mama said, rising from her chair.

Mary quickly covered the distance to her stepmother and embraced her. "I am sorry," she whispered.

I felt a pang of jealousy watching my cousin and mother embracing for the first time since the wedding, but I forced it away. It appeared Uncle Jacob wasn't the only one softening. *This is a day of surprises.* That night at supper, however, I learned the day held yet one more.

10
On the Road

"MY COUSIN'S SON IS GETTING MARRIED NEXT WEEK in New Market," Uncle Jacob announced at supper.

His sudden, awkward attempt at conversation surprised me. I glanced toward Mama and Mary. They also looked surprised.

"Oh?" prompted Mama.

"I thought we should go," he continued.

"We?" she asked.

"*Ja, ja*," Uncle Jacob replied, a hint of impatience in his voice. "All of us. The children, too. We can stay with Rueben and Sarah."

"Jacob, that would be wonderful fun." Mama smiled. "Do you not agree, children?"

"*Ja*, Mama," Leon answered. His eyes shining, he looked as if he were barely able to contain his excitement. Peter and Mary nodded with pleased smiles. Amos stared solemnly at his food.

We had not left our small town since arriving in Harrisonburg eight months earlier. I remembered Uncle Reuben and Aunt Sarah from Uncle Jacob and Mama's wedding.

"The wedding is Sunday. We will leave Friday morning and get there by Saturday night. We will stay until Tuesday morning. Plan to camp one night each way," Uncle Jacob said. "Elias Zook and his boys will take care of the livestock until we return."

The next days were filled with travel preparations: baking, laundering, packing, and sewing. All three of us girls had grown since our parents' wedding and needed new dresses, and Peter needed a new white shirt and black pants. The other boys could get by with hand-me-downs. For a wedding gift, Mama embroidered delicate pink roses on the edges of two plain muslin pillowcases.

Dependable Martha had agreed to help Grandma Clara with the household chores on Saturday. My anticipation of the trip lessened the disappointment I felt for missing a day with my grandmother. "I like your grandmother," Martha had said. "I think it will be fun to help her."

Soon Friday morning arrived. After chores and breakfast, Uncle Jacob and the bigger boys finished loading the wagon while Amos entertained Magdalena. Mama, Mary, and I hurried to wash and put away the breakfast dishes. Rushing from room to room, I grabbed last-minute items and worried over what we might be forgetting.

"Did you remember the blankets from your beds, girls?" asked Mama. "We will need those for camping."

"*Ja*," Mary answered. "They are already in the wagon."

"Did you notice how quiet Amos is? Do you think he's all right?" I motioned toward the window where my youngest siblings played outside on a wooden swing hung from a maple tree with thick ropes.

Mama stood behind me and looked out at the playing children. "I expect he is afraid of the wagon ride." Tears welled in her eyes. "It brings back fearful memories for all of us. He was the first to find your father after he was...after the accident." Her voice quavered. She covered her mouth with her hand.

My stomach roiled. The memory of my father's open, lifeless blue eyes intruded my thoughts. I shook my head, trying to erase the image.

"He has been stuttering again since we started planning this trip," Mary added. "It had been improving before then."

"I noticed that, too," I said.

Mama looked worried. "You are right. Can you girls think through our menu for the trip and make sure we have all the cooking utensils we need? I will go talk with Amos."

"*Ja*, Aunt Elizabeth," Mary said.

Mama approached Amos and knelt next to him. Soon he was in her arms, his face wet. Tears pricked my eyes as well, but Mary was talking to me, so I blinked them away and turned to listen.

An hour later, the wagon was full, and we'd already been traveling for half that time. Amos was quiet, snuggled securely in Mama's arms. Uncle Jacob, Peter, and Mary sat on the bench behind the horses. The rest of us nestled among the sacks and boxes of food, clothing, blankets, and other items needed for the six-day trip. The pots, pans, and other cooking utensils hung from hooks attached to the wooden framework holding up the wagon's cover. They banged together with loud clangs right above our heads as the wagon bumped and jolted over the rough road.

Magdalena stood and took two steps on shaky legs. "*Sit sie da do*, Magdalena," Mama said for the fifth time since we'd set out.

"I'll hold her. Come here, Maggie." I held out my arms.

I wanted to read, but the noise, cramped quarters, and jostling of the wagon made it difficult. Maggie lurched toward me and fell into my lap. I shifted uncomfortably and tried to stretch out my legs, but a box of food was in my way.

Although Mary and Peter were willing to take turns so the rest of us could sit up front with Uncle Jacob, only Leon, Mama, and Magdalena had done so. Amos and I stayed in the back.

During the long trip, we sang songs and told stories. Mary and Mama both attempted embroidery, but the jerking of the wagon resulted in several pricked fingers until they finally gave up for fear of staining their designs red with their own blood.

Three hours later, we stopped for lunch next to a shady brook. My legs were cramped and stiff. I limped out of the back of the wagon and stretched before finding a dense bush for privacy to relieve myself. When I was finished, I helped Mary and Mama get out our lunch provisions – bread, cheese, and cherries washed down with clear, cool water from the brook.

Afterward, we children took off our shoes and stockings and waded in the sunlight-dappled brook. Mama joined us.

The water was so cold my feet ached at first, but before long, I couldn't feel them anymore.

Tiny, silver-scaled fish flashed as they swam past our ankles, sometimes brushing against them, prompting Magdalena to giggle and shriek with glee. Leon, Peter, and Amos chased frogs on the bank.

I shuddered at the thought of touching a slimy frog.

Uncle Jacob, his hat over his face, lay in the grass and dozed while the rest of us played and the horses grazed.

I had never seen Uncle Jacob so relaxed. I breathed deeply, smelling wild roses and new grass, wishing the moment could last forever.

All too soon, Uncle Jacob sat up and announced it was time to continue. We knew better than to protest and obediently climbed into the wagon. The afternoon passed much more quickly than the morning as we all napped, our full stomachs and the rocking of the wagon lulling us to sleep.

"Whoa," Uncle Jacob commanded the horses. The wagon slowed and stopped.

"What's wrong?" whispered Leon, groggily. "Why did we stop?"

"Shh. I hear voices." I lifted Magdalena off my lap and crawled to a small hole in the canopy. My eyes blinked in alarm. I took a step backward.

"Susanna, do not eavesdrop." Mama frowned and gestured for me to sit down.

I sat and took Magdalena into my lap again. My voice trembled. "There are two men out there. They have guns."

11
Remembering

Mama rose and stepped up to peek around the edge of the canopy.

Uncle Jacob's voice maintained a firm, measured tone. "No, I have not seen him."

One of the men spoke again, and Uncle Jacob answered, "I will do what the good Lord requires." He signaled the horses to begin again, and the wagon rolled forward.

"What did they want?" asked Mama.

"Looking for a runaway." Uncle Jacob handed Mama a poster.

Mama sat back down inside the wagon, reading it silently. Her cheeks flushed red.

"What does it say?" I asked.

Mama read, "*Twenty-five dollars reward. Runaway from my place in Augusta County, Virginia, my Negro man Lorenzo Johnson, of black color, about five feet ten inches high, weighs about 175 pounds, and is probably hiring himself to cook. The above reward will be paid for his safe delivery to me at Preuitt and Company's office, or safe lodgment in some jail. He came from Staunton. Left home 15th February last. Alfred N. Preuitt."*

The wagon continued jostling as the pots chimed overhead, but no one spoke for several minutes. I remembered hearing about runaway slaves who had sought shelter in Pittsburgh. Not many slaves made their way to where I used to live in Lancaster County, but some accompanied their masters from time to time as they passed through.

"If Uncle Jacob sees that slave, will he turn him in?" Leon broke the silence timidly.

"No," Mama answered.

"But he said – I mean, I thought I heard him say – he told those men he would do what the Lord requires," Leon stammered, clearly upset.

"What do *you* believe the Lord requires?" Mama asked.

"That we not hinder a man's freedom," Leon answered.

Mama smiled.

"Oh." Understanding brought relief to Leon's face. "But why did he not tell those men that? Why didn't he tell them no?"

"Because he could be fined or even sent to prison for taking the position that men may not own other men," explained Mama. "That is a law in Virginia. Besides, it is not our way. Mennonites believe we are to separate ourselves from matters of the state. That way we are *in* the world but not *of* it."

"It is about time to stop for the night, but I want to get farther ahead, away from those slave hunters," Uncle Jacob called into the back of the wagon.

"That is best," Mama agreed. She closed her eyes and bowed her head.

"Are you praying for the runaway slave, Mama?" Leon whispered.

"*Ja.* I am praying for Lorenzo," she answered.

"I will, too." He lowered his head.

I joined them in their silent petition.

We rode for another hour, the mood solemn. Even Magdalena sensed the unrest the rest of us felt and was more subdued than usual.

"Welcome to Timberville," Uncle Jacob said as the wagon pulled into a small town surrounded by forest.

The town consisted of one dusty road lined on each side with modest storefronts and offices. Now that it was dusk, only one establishment appeared open. Rollicking piano music, bursts of laughter, and light poured from the windows. A wooden sign hanging above the door read "Riddle's Tavern." The wagon continued through town until it stopped near the bank of the Shenandoah River. We climbed out and stretched our cramped muscles.

"We will camp here and cross in the morning," Uncle Jacob said.

"Cross?" Mama asked.

"Cross the river."

Mama scanned the length of river before her. "But there is no bridge. Where will we cross?"

"We will go through it. The bridge washed away years ago, and they have not built a new one yet, so we have to make do and wade through."

Mama's eyes widened. "Is that not dangerous? Jacob, the children…"

"They will be fine. I know it is getting too dark to see it well, but the river is shallow and calm across here."

Mama's face relaxed slightly. The current did sound peaceful.

I smiled widely at Leon who grinned back. Crossing a river seemed like fun.

"Let us make camp. Peter, start a fire for us." Uncle Jacob reached into the back of the wagon and then he handed Peter a load of firewood.

We all helped to unload sleeping gear and cooking equipment. Even Magdalena kept busy, carrying smaller items to the spot Peter had selected for the campfire.

By the time we set up camp, the night was inky black except for a brilliant multitude of stars and the cozy fire. Mother had brought beef kept on ice cut from Lake Shenandoah during the winter and frozen in an underground icehouse near the creek at home. Now thawed, the beef mingled with carrots, potatoes, peas, turnips, and canned tomatoes in a kettle of bubbling stew hung over the fire.

My mouth watered at the smell, and my empty belly gurgled in anticipation as Mary filled the bowls.

"Do you suppose Lorenzo – that man who was running away – is all right?" Leon asked, blowing on his steaming stew to cool it.

"We can only pray that he is," Mama answered.

Mary looked thoughtful and asked, "Papa, I remember a woman…a black-skinned woman called Petunia. Who was she?"

Uncle Jacob raised his eyebrows in surprise. A shadow passed over his face, and his eyes hardened. "I need to tend to the horses." He stood abruptly, still holding his dinner bowl, and disappeared into the darkness.

Mary turned to Mama with a stricken look. "Did I say something wrong?"

Mama shook her head. "No. I am surprised you remember her. You were so young. Petunia nursed Peter and took care of both of you after your mother passed."

Peter's eyes bulged. "Nursed me?"

"You needed milk. Petunia had given birth to a stillborn infant girl. She was born dead, but Petunia still had milk."

Peter responded with an embarrassed grimace. "I need to help Papa," he mumbled. He stood and made a hasty retreat.

"How did Papa know about her?" asked Mary.

"He knew her owner. He owns a sorghum plantation up in Monterey."

"You mean she was a slave?"

"*Ja*, and your father had to pay for her. The church prohibits slave ownership, but they allowed him to buy her as long as he gave her freedom papers. He would have, anyway, so arrangements were made. Your father gave her a place to live and a small salary, and she agreed to stay until Peter was weaned."

"I remember she was sad. She cried a lot, but I didn't know why," Mary said. "What ever happened to her?"

"While she was taking care of you, her husband was sold south to a cotton plantation. I remember she feared for his life, but he escaped and moved to Canada. I was there when she got his letter, and I saw her smile for the first time. She had enough money saved by then to hire a stagecoach to take her to the nearest train with plenty left over. She had already begun weaning Peter, and it was not more than a week before he was feeding completely with a bottle. As far as I know, she is with her husband now in Canada, and Lord willing, she has children as well."

"Who took care of Peter and Mary after she left?" asked Leon.

"Oh, I helped when I could before we moved to Pennsylvania. Aunt Sarah came down from New Market for a time. Grandma Clara and Great

Aunt Ann did what they could. A few young women from the church helped...Lizzie Miller, Fannie Mae Troyer, Miriam Brubaker..."

"*The* Miriam Brubaker?" I asked. "You mean our *teacher*?"

"*Ja*. Actually I remember she helped quite often."

"She's the one I remember the best. She began teaching when Peter started school, but she took care of us a lot before then," Mary said.

The memories and the conversation slowed, finally drifting into silence as we sat mesmerized by the dancing flames of the campfire. Magdalena slept in my arms, and Amos, leaning against Mama, yawned and fought to keep his eyes open.

Uncle Jacob emerged from the shadows. Had he overheard our conversation? I studied his face for signs of anger. His eyes were somber, but his forehead was relaxed. He lifted Magdalena from my embrace, carrying her to the bedroll she and I shared. Soon I snuggled next to her under the stars, both of us warm under our quilt except for the tips of our noses.

The next morning, I awoke to the music of the nearby river and sparrows in the trees. A quick breakfast of biscuits and smoked ham was spread out on a flat rock. My stomach rumbled as I helped myself.

Mama was at the river's edge, washing the dishes that had only been rinsed the night before. Uncle Jacob was already harnessing the horses and loading the wagon. "Get up, Peter…Leon. I need your help."

As the boys scrambled out from under their quilts, I remembered the plans to cross the river. Smiling, I whirled around and dashed back to our sleeping spot. "Come on, get up!" I nudged Amos and Mary with my foot. Magdalena could sleep until we were ready to go. Packing up was easier that way.

After we loaded the wagon carefully to protect our possessions from the water, Uncle Jacob threw a stick in the river to test the current. Next he tossed in rocks "to test the depth," as he explained, listening to the telltale cracking sound of one rock hitting another at the bottom. Satisfied, he instructed the rest of us to sit in the back. "No standing," he ordered.

Once we were all seated, the wagon rolled forward.

The river sounded much louder as we entered it, the clamor of the rushing water roaring into my ears like a windstorm.

The horses faltered for a moment when the river licked their bellies, but Uncle Jacob snapped the reigns and ordered them on.

I crouched low in the wagon bed, the water splashing against the bottom. A thrill ran up my spine as moisture crept between the floorboards under my feet. I squealed.

Mary and Mama both looked queasy. Amos buried his head in Mama's lap, and Magdalena whimpered in Mary's arms. Leon caught my eye and grinned, his eyes shining.

The wagon stopped with a jolt and pitched downward at the front end. Frigid creek water sloshed over the front and sprayed us. The horses whinnied shrilly. Boxes slid forward. Peter and Leon lunged forward and stopped them. Two pots fell off their hooks, landing with a loud crash on the floorboards, one of them barely missing my foot. Magdalena flew from Mary's arms toward me, landing hard with a shriek against my hip.

"Magdalena!" Mary's face paled. "I'm sorry. I thought I had ahold of her."

I picked her up and held her close as she cried. "She'll be fine."

Amos's initial scream turned into great ragged sobs. Mama held him close, her head bent down over his shaking body.

"Jacob, *was iss los?*" called Mama.

"I think the front wheel is caught in a hole." His voice, muted by the sound of the burbling creek, was followed by a splash as he jumped into the water. "Hup!" he shouted to get the horse to pull while cracking the whip. "Hup!" The wagon rocked forward slightly as the horses strained, then rolled back again. Another snap from the whip. "Hup!" Another unrewarded rocking. The horses nickered in protest.

"Peter, I need your help," Uncle Jacob called. "There is a loose board under my seat. Bring it with you."

Peter secured the box he'd been holding in place before he grabbed the board from up front and jumped in next to his father.

After handing Magdalena to Mary, I pulled off my shoes and stockings and waded to the front, where the water came to my ankles. I held my skirt up and peeked out.

Uncle Jacob lifted a large rock out of the creek and dropped it next to the wheel. He used it as a fulcrum and the board as a lever to lift the wheel out of the hole. The wagon rocked as he worked.

The water came only to a little above Peter's waist as he stood in the creek. He pulled the reins to guide the horses forward. "Hup!" he shouted as the wagon rocked forward.

A few minutes later the wagon lurched upward and was level again. The water drained out through the floorboards.

"*Abatz!*" shouted Uncle Jacob. The wagon stopped rolling.

He moved the rock and positioned the board over the hole to prevent the back wheel from getting caught in it.

"Now, Peter!" he called.

"Hup!" Peter yelled.

The wagon rolled forward past the hole. Leon cheered.

I returned to where I'd been sitting next to Mama and Amos. Amos was still crying but quieter now. Magdalena sucked earnestly on her thumb. She was nestled in Mary's arms.

I rehung the fallen pots on their hooks.

Peter scrambled back into the wagon, shivering and dripping with creek water. I handed him a blanket. He draped it over his head and wrapped it around himself like a cape.

Uncle Jacob climbed up and shoved the board back into place before returning to his seat.

Soon the wagon heaved upward as the wheels once again rolled onto dry ground at the opposite bank.

"We made it," called Uncle Jacob.

"*Danke, Gott im himmel.*" Mama sighed while surveying our possessions for potential water damage.

After the brief river-crossing adventure, the second day in the wagon passed uneventfully, the monotony broken only for lunch and the occasional stretching break. The novelty of a long wagon trip and picnicking outdoors was losing its appeal.

"*Sit sie da do*, Magdalena!" Mama said with an edge in her voice after the toddler stood for the umpteenth time.

"I-I'm hungry," Amos whined.

"Shush. We will be there soon, and then we can eat," Mama answered.

"B-but I want to eat n-now!"

"*Abatz!*" Leon barked.

"*Dumkopf,*" Amos muttered.

"What did you call me?" Leon asked, glowering.

"That is enough," snapped Mama. "Both of you be quiet."

Finally, we stopped at a large white farmhouse with green shutters, surrounded by barns and other outbuildings. Fields of wheat and corn spread out behind it and to either side.

Mama smiled broadly. "*Kinder*, it is time to meet your cousins."

12
A WEDDING

BEFORE UNCLE JACOB FINISHED TYING THE HORSES to the gatepost, Aunt Sarah flew out the front door, followed by Uncle Reuben and their six children.

"Brother!" she cried, her arms spread wide. She hugged him tightly. She turned toward Mama. "Oh, Elizabeth, You are a sight for sore eyes." The two women embraced.

"Welcome, Jacob." Uncle Reuben shook his hand.

"*Danke*, Reuben. It is good to be back in New Market," Uncle Jacob said.

I had already met Uncle Reuben and Aunt Sarah at Mama and Uncle Jacob's wedding, but they hadn't brought their children. I felt shy in the presence of this group of strangers.

"Come, *kinder*. I want you to meet your cousins," Aunt Sarah said after she'd finished greeting each of us with a welcoming hug.

"This is Jacob, my eldest, named after my oldest brother," she began, placing her hand on the shoulder of a tall, dark-haired boy, resembling his namesake as well as my father.

Papa, Uncle Jacob's younger brother, had been kind, gentle, and funny. Like his brother he'd had dark hair and vivid blue eyes. If it weren't for Uncle Jacob's unsmiling countenance making him seem ugly, he would be a very handsome man.

"Jacob, do you remember Mary and Susanna?" Aunt Sarah asked. "You were probably only about six years old the last time you saw them. Peter would have been born by then, too, but he was only a baby."

Jacob shook his head. "I don't remember."

"This is Rebekah," Aunt Sarah continued. "She is almost a year older than you, Mary."

Rebekah smiled. "I'm glad to meet you."

The remaining four children were introduced one by one, oldest to youngest: Ruth, John (named after my father), Paul, and Anna.

I followed Aunt Sarah, Mama, and the other girls into the house to prepare supper while the male members of the family remained outside.

There was much to be done: unloading essentials from the wagon, feeding, watering, and brushing the horses, and the usual evening farm chores. The work was done quickly, and the boys had time to play before dinner. Leon and Paul, both eight, seemed as though they had been friends for years.

Amos preferred to follow the older boys around, although Anna was his same age. "Amos, do you want to play with me?" she asked from the open window, forlorn as Amos chased after Leon and Paul, ignoring her plaintive invitation.

The table was already covered with pies for the next day's wedding, and the air was filled with a delicious aroma of apples and cinnamon. Mama added clear glass jars of colorful canned fruits and a variety of pickles, her contribution to the wedding feast.

We ate outdoors, savoring our dinner of ham, corn on the cob, peas, dinner rolls, apple butter, and fresh strawberries with cream. The grown-ups used the maple wood table on the front porch. We children sat on the porch steps or on quilts laid out on the grass in the front yard.

Rebekah, Mary, Ruth, and I all sat together on one quilt. Rebekah and Mary were quietly discussing my cousin Jacob's admiration of a girl from church. I strained to hear their conversation, wanting to join in. Ruth, a year younger than me, chattered about the wedding, her friends from school, and the family's pets. I couldn't help but feel a little annoyed.

As we ate, water heated in a big pot on the stove in the summer kitchen behind the main house. It would be mixed with cold well water in a tin washtub for the first of many baths that night.

When it was my turn, I got a fresh batch of water in which to wash. Ruth and Anna were not so lucky; they had to share the water after I finished.

Bathing was accomplished behind quilts draped over ropes hung across the corner of the room. A kerosene lamp sat on the floor next to a wooden chair, its flickering light warming the dim corner. A hunk of lye soap rested in a dish next to the washtub.

After undressing, I scrubbed at a soiled place on my dress before draping it across the chair. I'd have to wear it home again before having a chance to thoroughly wash it. The water was only tepid. I lowered myself into the tub. Although the night was warm, I shivered as I scrubbed. I had to bathe quickly to preserve some heat for the other two girls who would share the water.

Dressed in a cotton nightgown after my bath, I slipped through the back door into the main house and climbed the stairs to the girls' bedroom. Anna and Magdalena were already asleep, their tiny bodies snuggled together in Anna's small bed, Anna's arm wrapped protectively around her younger cousin.

Ruth was lying on a bedroll on the floor, covered in quilts. "Mama said you and Mary could have our bed, and Rebekah and I would sleep on the floor, but I think it is more fun if you and I share the floor, is it not? It will be like camping." She smiled enthusiastically, patting the bedroll beside her.

"*Ja.*" I forced a note of cheerfulness. Inwardly, I rolled my eyes. Didn't she realize I'd slept on the ground last night? I climbed in next to Ruth, who had been kind and hospitable, after all. Ashamed, I stopped complaining to myself. As Ruth told a long, detailed story about how her friend's brother almost died in a hunting accident, I drifted off to sleep. I didn't hear the end of the story, and I didn't hear the older girls come to bed, either.

The next morning, I woke to high-pitched shrieks. Disoriented, I briefly forgot where I was until I saw Ruth smiling at me, leaning on one elbow. "Time to wake up, sleepyhead," she said with a smile.

"Good morning," I replied through a yawn.

Anna was clumsily attempting to brush Magdalena's tangled hair, the cause of the shrieking.

"Here, Anna. Let me help." I crawled out from the warm quilts and gently took the hairbrush from her.

After Magdalena and I were both dressed and our hair detangled and tucked into place, I carried her downstairs with me. Ruth followed us, her endless chatter filling my ears.

Rebekah and Mary, already clothed in their Sunday dresses covered with aprons, were helping Aunt Sarah and Mama prepare breakfast when the younger girls and I joined them. Grateful I'd been allowed to sleep in for once, I cheerfully helped serve hotcakes with maple syrup to the younger children. Church would begin in a little over an hour, followed by the wedding.

We all had to crowd indoors for breakfast; the grass outside was too wet with dew and the air too chilly to permit a morning picnic. With the pies and preserves loaded into the buggy, there was now room to use the table. It seated eight — enough room for the adults and the oldest four children, including me. However, when I saw Ruth's look of disappointment as she settled on the floor next to Anna, I decided to join her. Mama's knowing wink and smile warmed me as I moved my plate to the floor.

By mid-morning, we were settled in our seats in the bride's home, men and boys on one side, women and girls on the other. Without a meetinghouse, the congregation took turns meeting in each other's homes, and because a wedding was to take place, today the bride's family was hosting the church service. All of the furniture in the front room was moved into the adjoining bedroom, except for the chairs. Church members brought additional chairs as needed. The kitchen was laden with food for the wedding feast: fried chicken, vegetables, dressing, mashed potatoes, gravy, ham, relishes, canned fruit, cakes, pies, and cookies.

The service opened with prayer, announcements, and several hymns sung a cappella. Although hymnals were available, most of us knew the songs by heart. As the minister, Brother Lind, began his sermon, I was relieved to realize he was a gifted orator. This was not always the case due to the church's practice of choosing ministers by casting lots.

When choosing a new minister, members of the church nominated up to a dozen men for the position. After the nominations were made, the bishop placed a note with a black mark or brief message on it inside a hymnal placed on a table amongst others, one hymnal for each candidate. The man who randomly chose the book containing the note was appointed as minister, regardless of his talent or desire. This practice was called "casting of the lots" and occasionally resulted in unfortunate congregations suffering through poor speakers, sometimes for decades.

Brother Lind began his sermon by warning about the pain of broken vows and the importance of persevering in marriage. He said, like a garden, a marriage needed to be tended – fed with kindness and watered with forgiveness; the weeds of resentment, anger, apathy, and unfaithfulness plucked out as soon as they sprouted. Although the sermon was interesting, it was also quite long.

My eyes grew heavy, and I stifled a yawn.

"What is love?" he asked. The question hung in the air for a moment. "Most people describe it as a feeling," he continued, "but what does Scripture say?"

He opened the heavy black Bible in front of him. "Another word for 'love' is 'charity.' In First Corinthians 13, the Apostle Paul describes charity thus: *Charity suffereth long, and is kind; charity envieth not; charity vaunteth not itself, is not puffed up, doth not behave itself unseemly, seeketh not her own, is not easily provoked, thinketh no evil; Rejoiceth not in iniquity, but rejoiceth in the truth; Beareth all things, believeth all things, hopeth all things, endureth all things.*"

I thought of Mama. I remembered when she told me how she chose to love Uncle Jacob, despite his flaws. In light of this verse, I began to understand.

Brother Lind looked intently at the people gathered before him. "Brothers and Sisters, love is not merely an emotion that comes and goes according to your moods and whims, a constantly changing thing. Love is a choice to consistently treat another with the highest regard. This applies not only to marriage but to all relationships. Now will the happy couple please come forward?"

From opposite sides of the room, a young man and woman rose from their seats and joined in the center before Brother Lind.

I connected the relationships in my head and concluded that the groom was my second cousin, the son of my father's first cousin.

The bride was from another family, although like most Mennonites, probably distantly related in some way. She wore a simple blue dress, no different than an everyday dress although likely the newest. Her brown hair was tucked neatly into the traditional head covering – a white, finely woven, brimless cap with ribbons tied loosely in front, the same as all the other females in the room. Only her flushed cheeks and sparkling brown eyes set her apart as the bride.

Brother Lind asked the couple a series of questions to which they each answered "Yes" or "I will." He asked them to join hands and pronounced them husband and wife. After he invoked a blessing, the couple took their separate seats, and the congregation knelt in prayer. The service concluded with a final hymn.

The smiling bride appeared so happy that an unfamiliar longing to have my own wedding surprised me. Marriage was expected of me. The desire to teach remained, however. *If only I could do both...*

My stomach growled. It seemed as though I'd eaten breakfast only minutes ago, but I guessed several hours had passed by now, and I looked forward to the feast that would follow. I accompanied Ruth outdoors to wait. For once I was glad to be counted as one of the younger girls, even though I'd turned fourteen in April. There were so many women and older girls present that they required no additional help. I enjoyed the rare opportunity to anticipate a meal without having to help prepare or serve it.

13
Rescue

Mama could no longer keep her pregnancy a secret as her middle swelled along with the summer's heat. Although the trip to New Market had improved Uncle Jacob's mood for a time, his irritability increased as the days grew warmer.

Magdalena was intrigued by the idea of a baby growing inside Mama. Each day she patted Mama's rounded abdomen and asked, "Baby in there?" Sometimes her pats turned into angry hits.

At those times, Mama removed Magdalena's hands and said, "No. Be gentle, Maggie."

When Peter first learned of Mama's pregnancy, he hadn't said a word. He had grown quieter since that day, stealing furtive glances at her, anxiety etched in his expression.

Mary, on the other hand, could not hide her delight. Every day she showed Mama her progress on the crib blanket she was crocheting and suggested names for the baby. On the rare occasion I suggested a name, she curled her lip in disapproval.

Mama was in the summer kitchen finishing supper preparations as Mary and I set the table in the main house. Peter came inside from feeding the cows, his eyes red and his cheeks mottled. I silently nudged Mary and nodded toward Peter.

Mary looked up and sucked in a breath when she saw his face. Eyes wide, she whispered, "Peter, what is it? Did Papa whip you again?"

"No. It's Esther. She's dead," he choked out.

"Oh, I'm sorry," Mary answered. "I know she was dear to you. She has not been well since she had her litter. It was too hard on her. At least you still have the kittens."

Fresh tears leaked from Peter's eyes. "Father told me to drown them because they haven't been weaned yet. He says we have enough to do around here without adding the nursing of useless kittens."

"Oh, Peter," Mary said soothingly, reaching toward her brother.

Jerking away, he fled to his bedroom, Mary's hand left poised in mid-air.

I caught a glimpse of vulnerability and compassionate sorrow in Mary's eyes before she lowered her hand and turned silently back to the table.

"How long have you had Esther?" I asked.

"Since before Peter was born. She was our mother's pet, and Peter has not known life without her."

"I'm sorry. She must have been special to you, too."

"She was only a cat to me, but Peter loved her. Birthing kittens was too hard on her. It killed her like…like…Oh, Peter," Mary whispered, her face stricken with a sudden realization.

I understood as well. Uncle Jacob had ordered the motherless kittens drowned because they were too much trouble without a mother to care for them. Did Peter think his father had thought the same of him when his mother died shortly after his own birth? "Mary, I – "

"Never mind. It's not your affair," Mary said sharply.

Magdalena cried out, waking from her afternoon nap. I turned so Mary wouldn't see the heat rising in my cheeks and went to tend to my sister.

Later that night, unable to sleep in the hot bedroom, I tiptoed to the window to see if I could open it wider. Out of habit, I looked toward Aunt Lydia's barn. Three times now I had seen a lantern glowing from the barn loft's window. I'd come to long for it when I stared out my bedroom window on restless nights. It must mean something, but I didn't know what. Shimmering in the darkness, especially when the moon was concealed by clouds, it comforted me. When I saw it, I felt welcomed, less alone. It was a promise. A promise of what, I did not know. I only knew that whenever it glowed, my heart beat a little bit faster.

On those nights, I watched until a wagon approached in the darkness.

It was always the same routine: A man knocked on the door. Then Aunt Lydia emerged with a basket and accompanied him to the barn. A short time later, the empty wagon left, and Aunt Lydia returned to her house.

Martha had said Aunt Lydia disobeyed the church counsel. Perhaps the bishop wanted her to marry someone the way he pressured Mama to marry Uncle Jacob. She must have declined. Maybe she was in love with the man who visited her, and that was why she refused. I wondered if he was already married to someone else and had to sneak to her at night. But why would they go to the barn to meet? Was it to keep their affair secret from Skip? None of that explained the wagonload of straw.

For several nights after that, if I watched at the right time, Aunt Lydia walked between the house and the barn. Sometimes her brother Skip accompanied her, but most of the time she was alone. She often carried a basket. What was in it? I was full of questions but knew better than to ask. Tonight the barn window was dark.

What on earth? The figure of a boy moved among the shadows in the direction of Aunt Lydia's barn.

He briefly turned his face back toward our house, looking over his shoulder. A patch of moonlight revealed the face of Peter.

What is that little schnickelfritz *doing?* Remembering Peter's stories about their mysterious neighbor, I gasped as the unwelcome image of a witch-bird pecking out his eyes came to mind. I shook away the thought as he made it to the neighbor's barn, lifted the latch, slipped inside, and closed the door behind him. Did he know what secrets she hid in there?

My heart pounding, I stared at the barn door and willed him to come out. Instead, I was startled to see Aunt Lydia leave her house and approach the barn, carrying a large basket in both arms. *Run! The witch is coming!*

I turned quickly to look at Mary, wondering if I should rouse her or run downstairs to Mama. *No. I don't want to wake Uncle Jacob. Besides, she is not a witch. Only an old lady. What can she do?*

I stared at the barn, anxiety mounting as the minutes passed with no sign of either Peter or Aunt Lydia. Finally, the barn door opened, and I was surprised to see the two of them come out together, both holding something small in their arms. Straining my eyes, I could not make out what they were carrying as they walked together toward the woodshed attached to the side of the house.

Moments later, Aunt Lydia left the woodshed and went indoors.

No longer fearful for Peter's safety, unless Uncle Jacob caught him out there, I let out my breath in one long exhale. What business could Peter possibly have over there in the middle of the night? And against his father's orders to stay away?

A cool breeze gusted through the open window.

I shivered. I wanted to return to my warm bed but was compelled to keep watching until Peter was safely back home.

A short time later, Aunt Lydia emerged from the house again, carrying a blanket and a small kettle.

Witch's brew. I smiled wryly, even while I wondered why Aunt Lydia brought Peter refreshments in the middle of the night. She entered the woodshed.

I was sleepy. My eyelids grew heavy, and my head nodded as I waited to see what would happen next. I folded my arms on the windowsill and rested my chin on them. I intended to close my eyes only for a moment, but they remained shut, despite my best intentions to stay alert.

Low voices jerked me fully awake. I didn't know how long I'd slept, but now Peter and Aunt Lydia were standing next to the fence between the properties. Peter climbed the fence and began sneaking toward home as Aunt Lydia returned to her house.

I tiptoed back to bed, resisting the urge to confront Peter and demand an explanation. I would ask him tomorrow. I drifted off to sleep.

Milking cows with Peter the next morning, I had finally found the chance to ask about his mysterious visit to the Swartzendrubers' barn the night before.

"Esther's kittens," whispered Peter. "I couldn't drown them. I couldn't. Please don't tell Papa. If I hid them anywhere on our land, Papa would find them. But if they live at Aunt Lydia's, then I'll know they are safe, and Papa will never know I disobeyed him."

"Weren't you scared when she caught you in her barn? Wasn't she angry?"

"Well, at first I thought she was, and I was a little scared, but when I explained about the kittens, she said she would help me."

"What did she have in that big basket?"

"What big basket?"

"The one she was carrying when she went into the barn?"

"I didn't notice. She must have left it in there when we moved the kittens."

"Why did you move them to the woodshed?"

"She said they would be warmer there."

"Hmmm...I guess that makes sense."

"And then she brought them some warm milk. We dipped rags in it, and they sucked it from the cloth. She doesn't want me to disobey Papa, so she'll take care of them until they are big enough to hunt for their food. She said Skip could help, too. That's her brother."

"I know. I've seen him at church." I paused for a moment. "What was the barn like inside? Did you notice anything...odd?"

"What do you mean? It's only a regular barn."

"What are you two talking about?" Mary demanded as she entered the cowshed. She carried a basket of eggs.

"Aunt Lydia. Maybe she's not a witch. Maybe she's nice," Peter said.

"Papa said to stay away from her," Mary warned.

"But why? You know the reason, don't you?" Peter demanded.

"Never mind. Quit asking about it. Please." Mary's voice was pleading.

Peter scowled and kicked a clod of dirt. He grabbed two full pails of milk and headed to the springhouse, where we stored the milk in metal jugs to keep it cool until needed.

What was everyone trying to hide? What had Aunt Lydia done to upset the church? Did it have anything to do with the barn, or was that something entirely different? What was going on in there, anyway? Asking questions wasn't doing me any good, and my curiosity grew by the day. If I wanted answers, I had to find them myself. I pressed my lips together in a determined line. I knew what I had to do. Now I only had to wait until it was time.

14
The Kittens

Two weeks after Peter hid the kittens, a lantern burned in the neighbor's barn loft window. I lay awake in bed, my heart racing. If I wanted to know what was going on inside that barn, tonight was a good night to find out. My conscience nagged me, but I shook it off. I would take only a quick peek inside and come right back, almost as though I hadn't gone at all.

When Mary's breathing became deep and rhythmic with a gentle snore, I eased out from under the covers and tiptoed to the open bedroom window. A warm July breeze ruffled my hair. The light still glowed from the barn. I took a dress from the chiffarobe and pulled it over my nightgown as I passed through the hallway to the stairs.

Once outside, I tiptoed through the backyard toward the creek. A sneeze startled me as I passed Aunt Lydia's woodshed on the other side of the fence. I ducked behind a nearby apple tree, my heart beating fast. Aunt Lydia must be feeding the kittens. But why in the middle of the night? Shouldn't they be weaned by now?

A child's quiet murmuring told me it wasn't Aunt Lydia after all. I hopped over the fence, crept to the side of the shed, and whispered, "Peter?"

Silence answered me.

"Peter, it's Susanna. Don't worry. I won't tell. Can I come in?"

The door creaked open, and I slipped inside.

Moonlight glimmered through the panes of one small window. Stacks of fragrant-smelling wood lined the walls. On the floor near the door sat Peter, cross-legged, a tiny gray-striped kitten asleep in his lap. Two kittens, one black with a white face and the other an orange tabby, wrestled nearby. Another with gray stripes lapped milk from a saucer in the corner.

"Oh," I crooned. "They're so little." I sat next to Peter and picked up the black one. It mewed with a tiny squeak. I tucked it into the hammock created by my skirt when I sat cross-legged. It tried to climb out, lost its footing, and rolled over on its back, its paws swiping the air. I stroked the velvety fur of its soft, round belly. It grabbed at my fingers, its tiny claws extended. "Ouch!" I giggled.

"Shh." Peter frowned and put his finger to his lips.

I set the kitten on its feet, and it waddled away. The orange tabby pounced on it, and the wrestling commenced again.

The kitten drinking from the saucer took one last lick and then cleaned milk from its face by licking one paw and rubbing it across its nose. "They're weaned already," I said. "Aunt Lydia will probably move them to the barn soon."

"Probably." Peter's face was downcast. He stroked the kitten in his lap.

"How often do you come out here?" I whispered.

"This is my third time. I usually fall asleep before Papa does, but sometimes, like tonight, he goes to bed early." His lips pressed together in a sullen pout as his hard eyes wordlessly dared me to scold him.

I ignored his surly mood and nodded toward the kitten. "Say you found that one and your papa may let you keep it."

He shook his head, scowling. "He'll know it's one of Esther's. He'll whip me for disobeying him." He squinted up at me. "What are you doing out here, anyway?"

I hesitated before answering. "Promise you won't tell?"

"I won't tell if you won't," he said, gesturing to the kittens.

"Did you notice the light in Aunt Lydia's barn loft window when you were outside?"

"No."

"Well, look."

He stood, gently lifting the sleeping kitten, and peeked out the window. "*Ja*, I see it." He sat back down. The kitten woke and stretched its back, its tiny rear in the air. It yawned, its pink tongue curling, and then it resettled in Peter's lap and fell asleep again.

"Something is happening inside that barn tonight. Something secret. Something she's trying to hide. I want to sneak over and find out what it is."

Peter's eyes bulged. "I told you she's a witch! It's witchcraft."

I shook my head. "I don't think so. Martha said she's not a witch."

"Well, I think she is. Don't do it, Susanna. If my papa finds out…"

"He won't. I'll be really fast. You can be a lookout for me."

"I don't want to be a lookout. Please don't do it," Peter pleaded. "Papa said we are forbidden to go over there. He'll whip you. She must be hiding something bad."

I bit my lip. My shoulders slumped as I let out a resigned sigh. "Fine. I won't do it."

"I'm going in now," Peter said. "Are you coming?"

"In a minute."

He studied me with narrowed, suspicious eyes.

"I said I wouldn't go over there. What if we're caught coming back in the house together? It's best we go in one at a time."

"All right. Goodnight." He handed me the sleepy gray-striped kitten and disappeared through the door.

I played with the kittens for a few more minutes and then left, closing the door behind me. After hopping back over the fence, I turned to gaze once again at the lantern in the window. I shook my head and walked toward the house.

The back door flew open with a bang. I jumped. Uncle Jacob stood there, glowering at me. My heart galloped.

"I thought I heard something. What are you doing out here?" he demanded.

I gulped. "I-I was using the privy." My lie came out in a rush.

"The privy is on the other side of the yard." His voice was icy.

"I did use the privy. But-but then I saw a light. I walked over to the fence to see what it was. Th-that's all."

He strode past me to the fence and stood with his hand on his hips, looking at Aunt Lydia's barn.

"I thought I told you whatever happens on that property is none of your business."

"I know. I-I'm sorry. I thought maybe it was a fire or…" My voice trailed off.

"Get back in the house now." His voice had taken on an annoyed tone. "Don't let me catch you fooling around near her property again."

"*Ja*, Uncle Jacob." I dashed through the back door and up the stairs to the safety of my bed. Had Peter told him I was out there? No, Peter had a secret of his own to keep. He wouldn't betray mine. Or would he?

15
STORMY WEATHER

A LATE SUMMER STORM TOOK US ALL BY SURPRISE. After weeks of relentless heat, the clouds rolled in and purged themselves of a month's store of rainwater. As soon as the first drops fell midafternoon, Mama and I opened the windows and doors, delighted to replace the stale air in the house with a fresh, cool breeze.

"The wash!" Mary shrieked, running outside to the clothesline. I ran after her.

Holding her swollen belly, Mama stood in the doorway and shouted, "Use the summer kitchen. It will be cool enough to cook in the main house tonight."

After piling the damp clothing on the clean worktable in the dim summer kitchen, Mary and I strung two ropes between the hooks embedded on opposite walls and hung the laundry. The small window used for ventilation on the back wall was open, allowing a cross breeze to help dry the clothes when the front door was left open as well.

"We might as well take some things back to the house to make supper," Mary said after we had finished hanging the wet garments.

"I'll bring the spider." I lifted the heavy iron skillet with legs from its hook on the wall. "Mama's frying chicken tonight."

Mary gathered the big pot for potatoes and the long spoon. "We'll need these, too."

As we walked back to the main house, I glanced across the fence at Aunt Lydia's barn. It stood dark and motionless as if determined to hide its secrets. I shrugged. It was too early for the light to appear in the loft window, anyway. I would look again after dark. A pang of guilt washed over me. What Aunt Lydia did in there was truly none of my business. Uncle Jacob would be so upset if he caught me out there again. But I couldn't let it go. Peter had made it to the barn to hide the kittens. If he could do it, so could I.

Mama greeted us at the open back door, her face beaming with joy. "Is this rain not wonderful?" Just then, the sky lit up behind her.

"Lightning!" Mary said.

"Start counting," Mama said.

We counted together up to "one thousand fifteen."

BOOM! Thunder jolted the sky.

"About three miles away," I said.

"What dat noise?" Magdalena, her eyes wide, toddled into the room.

"That was only a little *dimmel*, sweetpea," Mama crooned. "Do not be scared."

"What dat is?" Magdalena's voice trembled.

"Thunder is the sky having a loud party," Mama said. "It is happy because it gets to rain after being dry for so long."

Another loud boom startled us. Mama laughed.

"I scared," Magdalena whimpered. Her face crumpled.

"Come sit in my lap." Mama settled into her rocking chair. "I still have a little bit of lap left only for you." Magdalena perched on Mama's knees, draping herself over Mama's round midsection and burying her face in Mama's neck.

"Would you like me to read you a story?" Mama asked.

Magdalena nodded.

"Susanna, please fetch my Bible." Mama smoothed Magdalena's hair away from her face. "I will read to you about Noah's Ark, Maggie. How does that sound?"

"Maybe there's a better choice for today, Mama," I said, handing her the Bible. "You know, the flood…"

"Oh, *ja*. Good idea, Susanna. How about the story of Daniel in the lion's den?"

A small, dripping boy entered the doorway. "W-we are coming in."

"Goodness, Amos. You look like you've been swimming in the creek with your clothes on," Mama said. "Mary, would you please get a towel for Amos? Better make that four towels. The others will need them, too."

"Uncle J-Jacob said the f-fence will have to wait," Amos said.

"Well, it cannot be helped. Where are the others?" Mama asked.

"P-putting away the t-tools."

Mary handed Amos a towel. "Go get some dry clothes on."

A few minutes later, the rest of the family came in.

"Do not get too comfortable, boys. As soon as this rain lets up, we are back to the fence," Uncle Jacob said gruffly.

For the next hour, Uncle Jacob paced the kitchen floor, watching out the open door as the lightning and thunder continued unabated, coming as close as two miles, before it drifted away and finally stopped. The rain continued, but not as heavily as before.

"Come, boys. Rest time is over. You had best put your wet things back on," Uncle Jacob ordered.

After a few minutes, the boys emerged from their bedroom, shivering in their damp clothes.

Looking at Amos, Uncle Jacob frowned thoughtfully. "Son, I want you to stay in and help your mother. Go put your dry clothes back on."

Mama smiled with silent gratitude as the older boys followed him back out into the rain.

By the time supper was over that evening, the rain had ceased, the silence a stark contrast to the constant drumming of the rain on the roof for the past five hours.

"Peter, it is your turn to fetch the cows. Do not fail to bring them all in like last time, or it will surely be the switch for you tonight," Uncle Jacob warned.

"Yes, sir." Peter rose from the table.

I had noticed, after Uncle Jacob ordered Peter to drown the kittens, something had changed in my cousin's eyes. He remained unfailingly obedient, and Uncle Jacob had not whipped him all summer, yet something cold and lifeless had settled itself behind Peter's gaze. I was concerned, and I suspected Mary was, too.

Busy washing dishes and tidying the kitchen, I soon forgot about my worries for Peter. In fact, I forgot about him altogether until Mama asked Uncle Jacob if he had come in yet.

Uncle Jacob walked to the bottom of the stairs and looked up, hands on his hips. "Peter?"

Silence answered him.

"Peter?" he repeated.

Leon called down the stairs. "Peter's not up here, Uncle Jacob."

"Have you seen him since supper?" Mama asked.

"No."

"What is taking him so long? He left at least an hour ago." Mama looked out the window.

Uncle Jacob stepped out the front door and called from the porch, "The cows are back. They are standing outside the cowshed, waiting for that *dumkopf* to let them back in. He must be playing somewhere in the rain puddles. I will have to take the switch to him tonight, mark my words."

Mama moved to the door and looked out. "The rain…" she said softly. Then with sharp urgency she cried, "Jacob, the creek. It is bound to be flooded."

Without waiting to reply, Uncle Jacob bolted from the porch, racing toward the creek. Mary, Leon, and I jumped up and ran after him.

The cows had been grazing on the other side of the creek in a valley with more shade. Peter would have to cross it to get to the cows. I fought panic as I ran, my heart lodged in my throat. No deeper than my knees, the creek had never seemed dangerous before, but as I reached the bottom of the hill on the south side of the house, the water roared as it raged against its banks.

Flooded with rainwater, the creek surged with fury, hurtling debris downstream.

Uncle Jacob saw him before the others did. "Peter!" he screamed hoarsely.

My breath caught as I spotted my cousin, a small figure with his arms raised above him, struggling chest-high through the middle of the raging torrent.

Just then a heavy tree limb, propelled by the rushing current, crashed into his side, and he lost his footing, sinking under the black water.

"Peter!" Mary shrieked.

I opened my mouth to scream, but in my terror, I could produce no sound. I ran to the water's edge.

Uncle Jacob plunged into the creek downstream from where Peter had sunk. He dove under.

Although Mary and Leon were screaming, all I could hear was my own blood rushing in my ears. *Please God…God, no. Please…*

Mary, Leon, and I ran along the bank, searching the creek's depths.

Uncle Jacob reappeared, standing up to his chest in the raging creek. He turned his head from side to side, frantically scanning the water.

"Peter!" he shouted.

Just then I glimpsed something white farther downstream under the churning, black water. It was caught on the branches of a long-ago fallen tree.

"I see something!" I shrieked.

Uncle Jacob climbed out of the creek, ran down to where I pointed, and jumped in.

A moment later he burst out of the water, holding Peter up. He pushed him onto the bank and then climbed up himself.

Peter retched up creek water.

By now Mary, Leon, and I had reached them.

Mary was wailing, "Papa…Peter…Are you all right? Are you all right?" She knelt on the ground next to them.

Wordlessly, Uncle Jacob grabbed Peter and wrapped his arms tightly around him. His back shook with silent sobs, and his features twisted in a look of grief and remorse. He opened his mouth as if to speak, but no words came.

16
Sister Brubaker's Secret

"I believe he is on the mend," Grandma Clara said, examining Peter's fingernails. After being tinged blue the past two days, they were now a healthy pink, and his breathing had relaxed some. She pressed her cheek to his sweaty forehead and nodded. "Fever's broke."

The day after Peter's near drowning, he'd caught a cold. Two days later, he was running a high fever and wheezing, his ribs contracting violently with every forced inhalation. "Lung fever," Grandma Clara said, examining him after being summoned by Uncle Jacob for help. "Mary, chop up some onions, quickly. Susanna, fetch a tea towel and some twine."

We rushed to do as we were told. Mama heated lard in an iron skillet. Once the onions were steaming, fried in the hot lard, she scooped them into the tea towel and tied it shut with twine. Grandma Clara pressed it to Peter's chest. Tears streaming from his eyes, he moaned weakly in pain while it burned his flesh. Grandma Clara wept silently alongside him.

When Peter's wheezing was at its worst, Uncle Jacob held him over a steaming pot of water with a towel draped over his head, careful not to let the steam burn him. I had never seen him act so tenderly toward Peter.

Two nights earlier, when I woke during the night, I was too worried about Peter to even think about spying on Aunt Lydia's barn. Instead, I peeked in on Peter and found Uncle Jacob alone with him. Peter gasped and wheezed in tormented sleep. Uncle Jacob's large hand held Peter's smaller one, his head bowed as his lips moved in a silent petition.

Three days after Peter fell ill, he breathed more easily, although he had a cough that nearly strangled him at times. Around the clock, Mama, Grandma Clara, Aunt Ann, Mary, and I had been tending to Peter, replacing lukewarm onion poultices with steaming ones, kept hot in the oven. Occasionally we made porridge and ground mustard poultice, but we quickly ran out of mustard and returned to onions.

"Here's some hot tea with honey, Peter. Try to drink some," Mama said.

Peter slowly sat up. After a brief fit of coughing, he took the cup. The steaming liquid sloshed as the cup tilted in his trembling hands.

"Let me hold it for you." Mary took it from him before he spilled it and lifted it to his lips.

Peter took a small sip and winced. "Too *hees*," he rasped.

Mary blew on it. Soon Peter was asleep, breathing noisily.

As Mama and Mary returned to the kitchen to prepare supper, Grandma Clara and I remained to watch over our patient in the small room permeated with the pungent aroma of fried onions.

"*Schul* starts tomorrow," I whispered.

"Oh, I had nearly forgotten," Grandma Clara answered.

"Do you think I should go? I mean, do you need me to stay and help with Peter?"

"I think we will manage fine if you go to *schul*. Peter is much better, and Mary will not be going, of course."

Having completed the eighth grade the previous spring, Mary was finished with school. I would now be in the oldest class, along with Martha and four other students, all boys.

"Do you not want to go to *schul* tomorrow?" Grandma Clara interrupted my thoughts.

"I don't know," I muttered, looking down as I picked at my cuticles.

"Are you worried about Peter or about Sister Brubaker?"

I looked up. "Maybe both," I admitted. I had complained about my teacher a few times while helping Grandma Clara with Saturday housework during the summer months.

"Do not fret about Sister Brubaker," Grandma Clara said. "I think you will find her a much more cheerful sort this time."

"Why is that?" I asked.

Grandma Clara only smiled and winked mysteriously.

"Grandma," I whispered harshly, "what are you not telling me?"

"You will see," Grandma Clara teased.

I crossed my arms in mock indignation and glared playfully at my grandmother, but a smile sneaked through my pursed lips.

Grandma Clara chuckled. "Of course you will have to tutor Peter until he is well enough to go to *schul*. We do not want him to fall behind."

"I can do that," I exclaimed with delight. Helping Peter would almost feel like being a real teacher. Peter stirred and murmured in his sleep, and I quickly clamped a hand over my mouth.

Grandma Clara was right. Sister Brubaker seemed like a different person when she greeted me at the door. Along with her customary "Will you be an obedient child today?" she had grasped my hands warmly and said, "Susanna, it is so good to see you back in my classroom. How is Peter?"

Like always, the day started with the Lord's Prayer. I was determined to pay careful attention to the sixth-grade work along with my own in order to tutor Peter when he was well enough to listen and learn.

After the children were dismissed at the end of the day, Martha waited while I copied the sixth graders' spelling words into my notebook to take home for Peter. Today it was homonyms, groups of three words spelled differently but sounding the same: cite, site, sight; reign, rain, rein; vane, vein, vain; and raze, raise, rays.

Sister Brubaker appeared distracted, even nervous as she rearranged the items on top of her desk, swept the already-clean floor, and retied her bonnet twice.

As I finished copying the words, a man entered through the back door. I recognized him from church – Tobias Miller, a widower whose youngest child, a daughter, had been in eighth grade with Mary the previous year.

His eyes briefly widened in surprise when he saw Martha and me. He cleared his throat. "Please excuse me. I thought you would be alone." He backed toward the door.

A pink flush crept up Sister Brubaker's neck to her cheeks.

"Er – rather – I thought school was dismissed," he stammered.

"*Ja*, well…" The flustered teacher smiled timidly at him, and then glanced at Martha and me, her cheeks aflame.

I gathered my books and lunch pail.

"Good-bye, Sister Brubaker," Martha and I called as we walked toward the front door.

"Good-bye, girls." She bit her lip and clasped her hands tightly together.

As we descended the porch stairs, Brother Tobias announced loudly enough for us to hear, "I-I brought some wood for the stove."

Martha and I smiled at each other and waited until we were out of earshot before bursting into giggles.

"Sister Brubaker has a beau," Martha sang.

"So that's why Grandma said she'd be more cheerful this year. She must have known." I grinned with both amusement and genuine gladness at this turn of events.

17
Sneaking Out

TONIGHT WAS THE NIGHT. A LIGHT SHONE IN Aunt Lydia's barn window, and the wagon with a load of straw would arrive some time before sunrise. My encounter with Uncle Jacob the night I visited the kittens in the woodshed with Peter had only dampened my curiosity for a short time. I had seen the light and the delivery of straw again since then, and my determination to discover the secret only became stronger.

The idea of sneaking in for a quick look no longer satisfied me. I would likely learn nothing that way. I had to see what the man brought into Aunt Lydia's barn and watch where they hid it. The next time I saw the lantern in the window, I would sneak to the barn and find a hiding place to spy until the wagon left.

I was being deceitful and disobeying Uncle Jacob. My plan was a downright sin. For the past month, I had tried to talk myself out of proceeding with this risky endeavor, but by now my curiosity was stronger than my conscience. *If Uncle Jacob would be more forthright about why he forbade contact with Aunt Lydia and if he would be more forgiving of her, I wouldn't need to sneak and spy.*

The knowledge that this was a flimsy argument flitted through my mind, but I pushed it aside. At least I wasn't involving Leon or Peter, as I'd considered initially. This would be my sin and mine alone.

Peter wouldn't help me, anyway. He had already told me he didn't want to be a lookout that night in the woodshed. I had been suspicious that he had woken his papa to tattle on me that night Uncle Jacob caught me outside, but he'd said he didn't, and I believed him. Uncle Jacob had woken on his own. Perhaps the creaking of the stairs roused him as Peter returned to his bedroom. That just showed he was a light sleeper. I had to be as silent as falling snow.

Magdalena, who now slept on a trundle bed next to the bed Mary and I shared, slumbered soundly. Mary was also fast asleep, her breathing deep and steady in the darkness. I would be gone and back without them ever knowing. My pulse raced, and a knot twisted in my stomach. Pulling a dark green dress over my white nightgown to better conceal myself, I carried my shoes outside before putting them on.

The October night air was crisp, and I was glad for the extra layer of clothing as I hurried behind the summer kitchen and over the fence separating the two properties.

Peter's kittens had grown but were still playful, frisking and chasing each other near the fence line. Although Aunt Lydia had moved them to the barn, they roamed the property, returning often to the woodshed.

The creek, meandering alongside me, curved behind Aunt Lydia's house and through the back of her property. I counted on its gurgling to muffle my footsteps until I was behind the barn. The black kitten with the white face followed me. Creeping stealthily, I was glad Aunt Lydia did not own a dog to alert her.

When I reached the barn, I stopped and pressed my ear to the rough wood slats forming the back wall. All was silent except the creek and an owl hooting in the trees beyond. I dashed the length of the barn on the side hidden from view of the house and peeked around the corner. Light streamed from one of Aunt Lydia's side windows, but nothing stirred except the kittens by the woodshed and the wind in the treetops.

I sneaked to the barn door, briefly in full view of anyone who might be looking out a window in my direction, lifted the latch, slipped inside, and closed the door behind me.

I was glad for the lantern in the window so I could locate the best place to hide. In the back corner, I spied a stack of wooden crates. Empty milk jugs stood before them, and a saddle lay on top. Away from the lantern, the corner was hidden in shadow. I pushed the crates out from the wall a bit more, but there was barely enough room for me to sit and wait with a clear view of the barn entrance.

Dust, disturbed by the moving crates, made me sneeze three times in quick succession. A fat brown spider, barely visible in the dim light, hung from its web in the crate before me. I gasped and scampered from my hiding place. Grabbing a nearby pitchfork, I caught the spider in its web on one of the tongs and carried it to the opposite corner. Shuddering, I rested the pitchfork against the wall and returned to my hiding spot where I sat down and sneezed again. The black kitten with the white face curled up next to me. I stroked its soft ears, grateful for the company.

I didn't have to wait long. Within an hour, horse hooves clopped and wagon wheels creaked down the drive onto Aunt Lydia's property and stopped in front of the barn doors. The kitten lifted its head and stared in the direction of the noise.

As my heart beat rapidly both in anticipation and fear of being caught, the doors swung open. A man stood in the entrance, his head turning from side to side as if he were looking for something. "Is anyone in here?" he called. "Lydia?"

I shrank backwards farther into the shadows, trying to make myself invisible. The kitten relaxed, rested its head on its paws, and closed its eyes.

The man listened to the silence for several long moments before returning to the wagon outside. He left the barn door open, but I couldn't see him. After a few moments, he returned with a lantern, its glow lighting up the inside of the barn, threatening to betray my hiding place.

I couldn't duck any lower but held my breath, afraid to make the slightest movement.

The man strode toward me, pausing at each stall to cast the lantern light over it, looking for something. Or someone.

The kitten lifted its head again. *Why did it have to follow me in here?* It would surely give me away. My knees and hands trembled, and my heart beat so loudly I was certain the man would hear it if he got close enough.

When he reached the stall closest to me and paused to look inside, I ducked my head down into my arms. The light swept over me, and I nearly cried out. All I could do was crouch and wait for him to discover me. I wondered who he was and what he would do when he found me. *Oh, why did I ever disobey Uncle Jacob?*

To my surprise, the man did not see me. I lifted my head to peek when the sound of his footsteps moved away. I let my breath out silently through my nose. The kitten yawned and began to groom itself.

The man approached the ladder leading to the loft, set his lantern on the floor, and climbed up. When he reached the top, he took the lantern from the window. His footsteps sounded above my head, walking from end to end. Dust trickled onto my face when he stepped directly over my head. I stifled a sneeze. Light seeped through the cracks above me. After a few minutes, he climbed back down with the lantern from the window, placed both lanterns on an overturned barrel near the door, extinguished the flame in one, and went back outside.

Good. He's leaving. My legs were cramped, and my back ached. I shifted my weight to a more comfortable position. I would wait until the creaking of the wagon wheels signaled he had gone and then sneak back home.

I was barely resettled when the man opened the barn doors wide. Startled, my heart skipped a beat. I shrank back into the shadows. It wasn't over yet. He returned to the wagon, climbed onto the seat, and drove it into the barn. After closing the barn doors, he lowered the back of the wagon and said in a voice scarcely above a whisper, "You can come out now."

My eyes flew open wide. *He saw me after all.* My heart thumped wildly in my chest and my breath grew shallow.

As I began to stand, something moved in the wagon, and I quickly crouched again. He wasn't talking to me.

A man with shiny black skin emerged from underneath the load of straw. Yellow strands of it clung to his hair and dirty, tattered clothes.

My eyes grew wide when he and the driver helped two small boys climb out after him.

Next a woman appeared, grasping the hand of the driver, followed by two more men, one of them taller than the first man and one of them older, his hair streaked with white.

These must be runaway slaves like Lorenzo, the man the slave hunters were looking for on our trip to New Market. They looked so weary. Unbidden tears sprang to my eyes as I watched the children. They were thin and dirty.

The driver grabbed the handles of two buckets, already full of water and waiting against the wall, and placed them in front of his horses. Speaking in hushed tones, he said to the bedraggled group, "I'll go get the stationmaster. She'll have some supper for you. Find the loose board in the back corner. You can go through that to the outhouse behind the barn. You'll find a washtub of water back there and a bar of soap if you want to clean up." He left through the barn doors.

"Come, children," the woman said as she led the boys toward the back of the barn where I hid. She spoke so quietly I had to strain to hear her.

I ducked my head until the woman located the loose board in the corner opposite my hiding place and pushed it aside.

"Mama, I'm hungry," the smallest boy complained weakly.

"Shh. We'll eat soon, child." The woman ushered the boy through the opening in the barn wall. The other boy and the girl followed. The three men remained in the barn, stretching and shaking out their cramped limbs.

"How you holdin' up, Charlie?" the first man out of the wagon asked the older man. "Missin' them tobacco fields yet?"

"No, sir," the old man replied in a raspy voice. "I'm doin' just fine without 'em."

The two younger men laughed.

While the men talked quietly and waited their turns for the outhouse, splashing sounds reached through the wall behind me as the woman and children washed. I strained to listen to their muffled voices but couldn't make out what they said to one another. After they returned through the loose board, the barn doors opened again, and Aunt Lydia, carrying a basket, entered with the driver.

"It was already unlatched?" Aunt Lydia asked. "*Ach*. I must not be so careless."

My breath caught for a moment. Uh-oh. I almost gave myself away.

The driver turned toward the assembled group, "This is your stationmaster, Miss Lydia."

"Welcome. You must be so tired," Aunt Lydia said softly. "How long have you been traveling?"

"Left the plantation three weeks ago, ma'am," the taller man answered.

"They've been my cargo for two days," the driver said.

"That is a long time under the straw," Aunt Lydia said. "You must be hungry, too. How does pork roast and boiled potatoes sound?"

"Sounds good to me," the older of the two boys answered.

Aunt Lydia chuckled and gestured toward the wagon. "Let's get this straw out of here."

The driver walked to the corner in which I crouched. As he approached, it seemed as if he looked directly at me. I held my breath, afraid to duck lest the movement catch his eye.

He stopped and looked around until he spotted the pitchfork leaning against the adjacent wall. He grabbed it and carried it to the wagon to scoop out the straw, tossing it to the side. Then he pulled a feed trough in front of the horses and filled it with oats from a burlap bag.

By now Aunt Lydia was unloading the basket. Besides the roast and potatoes, she set out bread and butter, green beans, peach pie, and two bottles of milk. The travelers groaned with delight.

The savory aroma of pork roasted with sage made my mouth water.

Once the wagon was cleared of straw, Aunt Lydia used the back as a makeshift tabletop and set the feast along its edge.

Opening a feed bag leaning against the barn wall, Aunt Lydia asked, "How many passengers did you bring, Conductor?"

"Six," the driver answered.

Aunt Lydia pulled seven plates, cups, knives, and forks out of the feed bag and distributed them to the travelers, including the driver.

After they'd all filled their plates and sat down, the old man said grace. They all murmured "Amen" before beginning to eat.

"While you are eating, I will tell you what you need to know. You will sleep in the loft above you. The ladder is there." She pointed. "When you go up, you will see hay bales forming a wall along the back. On the left is a small opening through which you can enter a hidden room behind the wall of hay. There are two sets of bunk beds up there, with an additional mattress for someone to sleep on the floor, and plenty of blankets.

"Under the beds are boxes with clean clothes and shoes if you need them. I will wash your things tomorrow if you leave them in this barrel here." She tapped a barrel beside her. "My brother Skip will replace the water in the washtub each morning. I will serve three meals a day. Breakfast is at eight o'clock."

The visitors listened as they ate, clearly famished. The food smelled delicious, and my stomach grumbled. I stifled another sneeze; fortunately, Aunt Lydia had barely paused between sentences, and her words masked any wayward noises I made.

"You will stay here for two nights more after this one. On Thursday you will leave after nightfall and travel on foot. I will bring you cut red onions to rub on the soles of your shoes to throw off any dogs that might come looking for you.

"You will leave through the loose board in the back and run along the creek. Just past the orchard you'll see a shallow place to cross. Then run north through the wooded area beyond. When you come to the next clearing, stay hidden in the trees until morning. Before daybreak, a wagon will pass by.

"Your new conductor will be wearing a brown, broad-brimmed hat and a black overcoat with a red scarf. He will be whistling a tune. When you hear him, make the sound of a mourning dove." She demonstrated the call. "If he replies with the same dove call, step out into the clearing, and he will pick you up and take you to the next station. We will go over all this again before you leave. Do you have any questions?"

They shook their heads. "No, ma'am," the taller man said wearily.

"Well, then," Aunt Lydia said, smiling at the conductor, "I guess there is only one thing left to do."

I gasped as the conductor opened a pocketknife and walked toward me. He stopped abruptly and stood still. He turned his head slowly from side to side, his posture rigid. This time I had no doubt. He must have heard me. I covered my mouth with my trembling hands, afraid to breathe.

Just then the kitten stood, stretched, and jumped up onto the saddle perched on top of the crates I hid behind.

The man shook his head, chuckled, and walked to a support beam five feet in front of me. He carved six notches into the wood where they joined dozens of other similar marks. I allowed myself to breathe again.

When he finished, he solemnly shook the hands of each of his travelers, even the children, and wished them God's blessing. Climbing into the seat of his now-empty wagon, its tail end upright and locked into place, he said to Aunt Lydia, "The next load will arrive in late December if all goes as planned. I'll keep in touch."

"*Gott segen eich*," she replied as she swung open the barn doors.

"God bless you, too," he said as he backed the horses out.

A growing realization hit me. That was why the church ignored Aunt Lydia. Although she wasn't doing anything morally wrong, she was directly disobeying the law. She was doing something right and good, but by doing so, was making herself "of the world" by becoming involved, something the church taught against. I didn't know if I should admire her or avoid her like the others did...like Uncle Jacob ordered his family to do. Surely he knew about this.

I crouched in my hiding place until everyone had used the outhouse, washed, and climbed up to the loft, taking the lantern from the barrel with them. Its light sneaked down through the loft's floorboards. Voices murmured above me. The lantern went out, and I was left in complete darkness. By the time my eyes adjusted, at least two people were snoring in the beds overhead. I waited a bit longer, feeling sleepy myself.

Confident they all were asleep, I crept from my hiding place and took hold of the loose board, glad for this less conspicuous way to leave. The board creaked slightly as I moved it.

One of the snores stopped abruptly.

I froze, afraid to even breathe. Dust tickled my nose as I desperately stifled the urge to sneeze.

After a moment, the snore resumed.

I let out my breath and crept out the opening, through the night's shadows, to my own house and waiting bed.

I lay in the darkness, the faces of the children sleeping in the barn filling my thoughts. Aunt Lydia helped runaway slaves. The church knew and disapproved, avoiding her as a consequence. Even Grandma Clara stayed away from her. But wasn't Aunt Lydia doing the right thing? After all, if God cares for fallen sparrows, as Grandma

Clara said, how much more must he care for the people I saw tonight? *I want to be like her. It doesn't matter what anyone thinks.* Martha's face flashed into my mind before I fell into a restless sleep.

18
A New Arrival

"Susanna, the ash box needs to be emptied," Mama said as I entered the warm kitchen from the back door, my arms laden with kindling.

"*Ja*, Mama."

As I turned toward the black, cast iron stove, the sound of water splashing on the floor along with Mama's surprised "Oh" caused me to glance back. A puddle grew under my mother's skirt.

"The baby!" I exclaimed.

"*Ja*, my water broke. Run and get Jacob."

I raced out the back door. "Mary, the baby's coming!"

Mary, leaving the woodshed, dropped her load of kindling and hurried into the house.

I found my stepfather in the stable scraping Old Tom's hooves while Peter, Leon, and Amos mucked out nearby stalls.

"The baby's coming," I blurted when I saw him.

His eyes widened, and he instantly dropped the hoof pick and rose to his feet. His mouth set in a grim line, fear clouding his features.

My stomach clenched.

He gestured toward a chestnut-colored mare gazing indifferently from another stall. "Peter, take Nellie and fetch your grandmother."

He turned to the younger boys. "Leon and Amos, when you have finished mucking the stalls, you had best come in and go straight to your room."

I followed Uncle Jacob as he rushed toward the house. Inside, Mama lay on top of a thick, worn quilt Mary had placed on the bed to keep it clean.

Mama's face was already flushed and shiny, her eyes closed and lips parted. Mary sat anxiously next to her, a solemn Magdalena on her lap.

"Elizabeth?" Uncle Jacob's voice cracked.

Mama opened her eyes and smiled weakly.

"It has started, Jacob," she said. "*Ach*. Do not look so worried. I will be all right. The baby, too. Is Clara coming?"

"I sent Peter for her." He reached for her hand but stopped when he saw the dirt covering his own. He turned to me. "You had best boil some water or something. And take Magdalena out." He rubbed his hands vigorously on his pant legs in a futile effort to remove the dirt on his palms.

Although I didn't want to leave Mama's side, I also didn't want to stand idle. I disliked feeling helpless. Reluctantly, I returned to the kitchen and grabbed the water buckets near the back door, heading out into the chilly November air toward the pump. I was glad it was Saturday, or I might have come home from school to discover a new baby had been born while I was gone.

Grandma Clara and Aunt Ann arrived as the water began to boil. Jacob bent down and kissed Mama's perspiring forehead. "Take care of her, Ma." He left the room, leaving the child-birthing business to the women.

Mama, seized with a contraction, cried out. Grandma Clara and Aunt Ann immediately went to work.

I let out a deep breath, knowing their years of experience had taught them exactly what to do. Mary and I hovered nearby, entertaining Magdalena and fetching towels, water, and other items required by the midwives.

As the afternoon labor stretched into the evening, we took a break only to set out a quick meal of bread, cheese, and canned fruit. The younger children ate quickly with fearful eyes as Mama's groans and cries of pain reached our ears at one-minute intervals.

"It's almost time," whispered Mary.

The two younger boys nodded nervously. Peter sat hunched over with his head in his hands. Uncle Jacob paced, too anxious to sit. Only Magdalena had an appetite, too young to fully understand what was happening in the next room.

Aunt Ann briefly opened the bedroom door and announced, "She is crowning. We see the baby's head."

Mary and I leaped up and rushed to the room.

"Push, Elizabeth," instructed Grandma Clara.

Mama curled forward, her face straining as she gasped in pain and effort. After the contraction passed, she lay back again, panting.

"Mama..." I said, taking her hand.

"She cannot talk now," admonished Aunt Ann.

Mama squeezed my hand when the next contraction hit. Her grip tightened as her groans grew louder. My hand throbbed. After several long moments, she relaxed her hold and fell back against the pillow, sweat beading on her brow.

"Here she comes – or he." Grandma Clara leaned forward to ease out the baby's head. "One more push should do it."

Mama still held my hand. I braced myself for another painful squeeze.

Finally, the slippery infant lay motionless and silent on the bed, still attached by his umbilical cord. Picking him up by the ankles, Grandma Clara hung him upside down and slapped his bottom. The newborn took a sudden breath and let out a thin wail.

"It's a boy," Mary yelled out the door to her pacing father.

Aunt Ann clucked, "*Du armes kind. Dass du auch musst zu dieser verkrüppelten Welt geboren sein.*"

"Now, Ann," Grandma Clara scolded as she swaddled the wailing infant in a length of ivory flannel, "you may be right that this child was born into a crippled world, but you needn't call him 'poor.' His belly will be content, and he will be well loved. That's all anyone needs to be truly rich."

Smiling, I gazed at my new brother, his tiny face wet and wrinkled, and whispered "Joshua," the name the family had chosen for a baby boy.

19
Unintended Consequences

"What is this?" demanded Uncle Jacob angrily, glaring at Mary. He had just returned home from town on a Friday afternoon holding an open envelope.

I looked up from the table where I was helping Amos with his arithmetic assignment. Magdalena played with a rag doll at my feet.

Bright pink stained Mary's cheeks, and she stammered, "You-you opened my letter?" Her voice rose into a squeak. "That was for me."

Joshua, now three weeks old, stirred in his cradle against the wall next to the back door. He'd been placed under a window in hopes the sunlight would cure his jaundice.

"You are going to wake the baby. I just got him to sleep," warned Mama wearily.

The fatigue lines in Mama's face deepened. Every night since his birth, Joshua had woken her and Uncle Jacob repeatedly, making them both tired and irritable.

"What is this all about, Mary? I thought you volunteered to collect the mail in town out of the goodness of your heart. Now I learn it is to sneak around like a harlot." Uncle Jacob said through narrowed eyes. Although his voice was quiet, hot anger bubbled just under the surface of each measured word.

Amos discreetly took Magdalena's hand and led her out of the room.

"I'm not a harlot," Mary cried. "I've done nothing wrong."

"Why is Benjamin Hostetler sending you letters? And do not even try to lie to me. I know this is not the first. The postmaster told me you have been receiving them since summer."

"We-we became friends when we went to New Market for the wedding. We are only friends, Papa."

"Where are the other letters?"

"In my room," Mary replied, her voice shaky. She looked at the floor, her cheeks glowing.

"Fetch them."

Shoulders slumping, Mary reluctantly climbed the stairs to the girls' room.

"Jacob, she is growing up. She is bound to have young men interested in courting her," Mama soothed. "She will be of age to marry sooner than you think. I remember Benjamin. He is Jonas and Fanny's son. He is a nice boy."

"If he were a 'nice boy' as you say, he would have written to me first, asking permission to court my daughter."

"He did," Mary said timidly. She had come down the stairs, clutching a stack of envelopes, wrinkled and torn by frequent handling. "Here it is."

Her father snatched the envelope from her outstretched arm, pulled out the letter, and scanned it briefly. "Why did you hide this from me?" His voice boomed, "How *darest* you?"

At this, Joshua fussed in his cradle.

"Give me the others." Uncle Jacob stretched out his hand.

"Papa, please," Mary pled, hugging them to her chest. "I didn't show you the letter because I was afraid you wouldn't allow it."

Grabbing her arms, Uncle Jacob wrenched the envelopes first from one hand and then the other and strode toward the woodstove.

"No, Papa. Please." Tears streamed down her cheeks.

Joshua began to cry in earnest, his wails urgent and high-pitched.

"I forbid any more contact with this boy, Mary." Uncle Jacob threw the envelopes into the smoldering stove. "That is your punishment for deception. I will write to this Benjamin Hostetler and tell him myself, and his father as well."

Mary sank to the floor on her knees, weeping silently in contrast to Joshua's loud cries.

I knelt next to her, laying my hand on her back. She didn't jerk away as I expected, but instead turned toward me, burying her face in my neck.

"I love him," she whispered.

"You have shamed me for the last time." Uncle Jacob's voice rose. "I am getting the switch. Maybe I can beat some respect into you." With a look of disgust, he stormed through the back door and slammed it shut behind him. Instantly, the baby's wails ceased in mid-cry.

Alarmed, I looked up as Mama rushed to the cradle. She stopped short and screamed. Mary and I hurried across the room as Uncle Jacob burst back in through the door.

"*Was iss letz?*" he shouted.

Mama screamed again. Mary's first sampler, a cross-stitch of the alphabet, had fallen from its shelf above the window when the door slammed. A corner of its heavy oak frame had landed squarely on the baby's soft temple. As Mama lifted the frame off the still and silent infant, blood streamed from the wound.

"What have I done?" cried Uncle Jacob, his voice cracking in despair.

"Wake up, Joshua. Wake up, precious baby," Mama pleaded as she carried him to the table with trembling hands and laid him gently on a dish towel. She placed her ear to his chest. "His heart beats."

"Susanna, tell Peter to saddle up Nellie and fetch Grandma Clara," Uncle Jacob ordered.

I rushed toward the door.

"No. That will take too long." Mama's voice was terse, forceful. "Get Lydia next door. She will know what to do." She bent down over the still, tiny body, covering his wound with her hand.

"No! I will not have that woman in this house. She could not save Rachel," Uncle Jacob protested. "She is no healer."

"She *is* a healer," Mama shouted, slamming her hand on the table. It left a bloody print.

Startled, we all turned toward her, our eyes wide. Never before had she raised her voice.

"Rachel could not be saved, or Lydia would have done it. This is no time for your stubborn pride, Jacob. She is our best hope." Mama glared at him.

Uncle Jacob's glowering eyebrows rose in surprise. He frowned and opened his mouth to speak but quickly clamped it shut again. He looked at the baby, and his shoulders dropped as he released a ragged sigh. "Get-get Lydia," he rasped, barely above a whisper.

I hesitated, uncertain if I heard him right.

"Get Lydia now," he snapped. "*Schnell!*"

I flew out the door and clambered over the fence onto Aunt Lydia's property.

Peter emerged from the barn with Leon where they had been tending to the horses, oblivious to the drama in the house. "Hey! Where are you going?" he yelled.

Ignoring him, I rushed to our neighbor's back door and pounded it with my fist.

Aunt Lydia opened the door. "My goodness. What is this all about?" she asked.

"My baby brother – please come quickly – he's hurt," I gasped.

"What happened?" Aunt Lydia asked.

"A picture frame fell on his head. It's bleeding. His heart beats, but he won't wake." My voice rose in a squeak as the tears came.

"Oh, dear. Skip, I am going to the Stutzmans' next door. I do not know when I'll be back." Aunt Lydia hastily gathered bandages and honey before following me out the door.

If I hadn't been so worried, I would have found the looks on Peter and Leon's faces amusing as they watched our plump, older neighbor climb over the fence, grunting and clinging to my shoulder for support. Going up to the road to get around the fence would have added precious minutes we couldn't afford, and after hearing the story, Aunt Lydia agreed.

As we approached the house, I heard a sound I never before would have been glad to hear – the urgent, piercing wails of a baby. Now it was the most beautiful sound I'd ever known.

Mama cradled Joshua in her arms, a tea towel pressed to the wound on his head. Although he smelled of sour milk, and dried blood already had crusted on his face, I felt a desperate urge to hold him, to feel his angry cries reverberating against my chest, proof he was alive.

Uncle Jacob stared at Aunt Lydia as she walked toward the baby. Fear and mistrust registered in his eyes.

Aunt Lydia glanced at him, and her steps faltered. Then she looked away and reached out for Joshua.

"Let me see, love," Aunt Lydia cooed, taking the baby from Mama. "Fetch a cold, wet cloth for me, dear," she instructed Mary, "and then heat some water, please."

Mary's expression was strained, her face streaked with tears. She looked at her father, who nodded his assent. She grabbed a clean dish towel and pail and rushed outside for water.

As Aunt Lydia gently wiped the blood from Joshua's forehead and covered the wound with honey and a clean bandage, the baby's wails turned to ragged breaths.

Uncle Jacob watched helplessly from a dark corner, misery etched on his face.

"What happened?" Peter asked as he and Leon entered the house.

"Joshua had a little accident. He'll be okay. Won't he, Aunt Lydia?" I asked.

"Lord willing. Would you light a candle for me, please?"

I did as I was told and took it to Aunt Lydia who held it in front of the baby's eyes.

"That is good," she said. "His pupils are even. I suspect it is only a surface wound. Keep watching him tonight to make sure he breathes normally. Check his pupils now and then."

"But what happened?" Peter demanded.

No one answered. I met his gaze, frowned, and shook my head in a silent warning.

"It is my fault," Uncle Jacob groaned from the corner. "I am...a wretched man."

"Oh, Jacob, no. It was an accident," Mama soothed.

"Where are Amos and Magdalena?" Leon asked.

"Check the chiffarobe," I said. "They are probably hiding." It had been so long since I had felt the need to hide that I had nearly forgotten this sad ritual.

"Slamming the door in anger was no accident. My temper is to blame. It is so monstrous that children hide from me." Uncle Jacob stood. "I do not deserve this family."

He took his hat and coat from a peg near the door and put them on. He looked at the floor. "*Danke*, Lydia." His voice was tight, defeated. "*Danke* for coming." Shoulders hunched, he left through the parlor and out the front door.

"Where's he going?" Peter asked.

"I do not know," Mama answered, her face lined with anxiety. She changed Joshua's soiled clothes, carefully pulling his bloodstained undergarments over his head so as not to scrape against the wound.

Leon followed me to the girls' bedroom. Sure enough, Amos and Magdalena were hiding inside the wooden closet.

"Is-is it over?" Amos whispered, wide-eyed. Magdalena had fallen asleep.

"*Ja.* Everything will be okay," Leon said. His voice was reassuring. He sounded so grown-up for a boy who had only recently turned nine.

I wished I felt as confident as he appeared. I woke my little sister, and we returned to the kitchen.

Amos and Magdalena blinked and squinted in the well-lit room after hiding in the dark chiffarobe for so long.

"Lydia, I am afraid. Can you stay for a while?" Mama asked.

"Of course, dear. Would you feel better if I slept here tonight?"

Relief flooded Mama's face. "Would you?"

"Certainly. I will go home and fetch some of my belongings," she answered. "But I could use some help carrying things back." She looked at me. "Could your daughter come with me?"

"That would be fine," Mama said. "I'll have Mary *redd up* the bed in the girls' room for you."

Smiling, I stood. "I'm Susanna," I said, as we left through the front door.

"*Ja*, I know. I knew you when you were a little girl. Your grandma often speaks fondly of you," Aunt Lydia replied.

I was surprised, unaware they talked to each other. "You and Grandma are friends?"

"Well…not like we used to be. We were closer as children," she answered.

I didn't ask for an explanation. The church's disapproval of her aid to the runaway slaves must have had something to do with their cooled friendship.

We walked to the road and around the fence, allowing time for Aunt Lydia to share a funny story about Grandma Clara's encounter with a mouse in an outdoor privy when she was a young teenager. "She was not done with her business yet, so all she could do was sit in there and holler. I expect they heard her all the way to Richmond."

I giggled, delighted by the image of my grandmother as a girl my own age.

Inside Aunt Lydia's house, her brother Skip sat at the kitchen table, bent over an elaborate charcoal drawing of a bird. About fifty years old,

Skip had thinning blond hair flecked with gray, trailing over his small ears. Thick spectacles slid down his flat nose when he looked up at his sister with blue, slanted eyes. He pushed up his glasses with a stubby forefinger and smiled brightly when he saw her, exposing a gap between his two front teeth. A smudge of charcoal remained on the bridge of his nose.

"Liddy, you are home," he cheered thickly as if celebrating her return after a long journey. "I am almost finished. Look." He held up the drawing of a sparrow perched on a fence, his charcoal-blackened, short fingers grasping the sides gently.

"Marvelous, Skip," Aunt Lydia said. "This here is Susanna Stutzman from next door."

"Glad to meet you." Skip glanced at me and quickly averted his eyes to look bashfully at his artwork.

"That is a nice drawing, Skip," I said. "You are a good artist."

"*Danke*," Skip replied before returning to the table to fill in more background detail.

"Skip, I will be spending the night with the Stutzmans to help with the new baby. There is bread in the sideboard and cheese and apples in the cellar. Can you make do with that for supper tonight?"

"*Ja*, I'll be fine," Skip drawled confidently.

As Aunt Lydia busied herself gathering a few belongings and quickly setting the house in order, I whispered, "Will he be okay by himself?"

"Skip? Oh, heavens, *ja*. He is simple-minded but not like a baby," she explained. "I can leave him alone for a night now and then. He is actually quite handy and a help to me, and he keeps me company."

Uncle Jacob still was not home when we returned to my house. Mama nursed Joshua in her rocking chair; Magdalena pouted at her feet, complaining that there was no room for her on Mama's lap. Mary had begun preparing a supper of ham with potatoes and had set Peter to peeling them. Leon sat at the table with Amos, helping him finish his arithmetic homework.

"Did you see Papa?" asked Mary anxiously.

"No." I set Aunt Lydia's satchel on an empty chair.

"Lydia, will you look at him?" Mama removed Joshua from under the small blanket draped over her shoulder.

Aunt Lydia carefully lifted the sleeping baby into her arms and listened to his peaceful breathing. "He sounds healthy. I think we should let him sleep. When he wakes, I will look again at his eyes. Shall I lay him in his cradle?"

"*Ja, danke*," Mama said as Magdalena, sucking on the hand of her rag doll, climbed into her lap.

I looked up at the shelf above the cradle. It was empty, the sampler leaning against the opposite wall.

Although we set a place for Uncle Jacob, his chair remained unused throughout supper and even as we children went to bed.

Mary and I left our bed for Aunt Lydia and got out bedrolls to sleep on, which still smelled faintly of summer when we camped outdoors on our trip to New Market. We spread them out in the corner at the foot of Magdalena's little bed. Aunt Lydia had chosen to keep company with Mama, who wanted to wait up for her husband.

That night I dreamed about the wagon accident that had killed my father. A hornet buzzed around my head, the hornet that stung one of our horses, Old Tom. Only, in my nightmare, the hornet was as large as a cat, its stinger a foot long. The horse twisted and bucked, startling the others, and they all panicked to get away. The wagon tumbled and rolled on its side. Our possessions – dishes, food, clothing, furniture – hurled about me in slow motion, along with my brothers and sisters, including baby Joshua who was not yet born at the time of the accident. The final image was the lifeless blue eyes of my father.

I awoke with a start, my sweaty nightgown plastered to my body. I got up and tiptoed to the opposite corner of the room, muffling my sobs with my pillow because I didn't want to wake the others.

I'd woken in the wagon after it came to rest on its side, the horses standing still, now calm. Leon was shaking me and crying, blood seeping through his sleeve. Magdalena, with a cut on her forehead, howled in pain as Mama soothed her.

"John?" Mama called. Silence answered her.

I sat up, aching and dizzy, and climbed out of the wagon.

My father lay on the ground. Amos sat next to him, trembling silently, his eyes wide, staring at Papa's face. I took a closer look and shrieked.

Mama climbed out, holding Magdalena who was still wailing. When she saw Papa, she crumpled to the ground. Sobbing, I caught Magdalena as Mama fell.

Leon's face appeared through a tear in the canvas. "What is it?" he cried.

"Stay inside," I answered. "Here, take Magdalena." I handed her to him and walked to Amos.

Kneeling down, I wrapped my arms around him and turned him away from Papa.

"Are you hurt?" I asked.

He didn't answer. He did not speak again until after we'd been in Harrisonburg for a month.

The rest of that afternoon was only a blur now. I carried Amos to the wagon and told Leon that Papa was dead. I covered Papa with a blanket and waited for help, not knowing what else to do. I could still hear Mama's wails after she woke.

A passing traveler named Coot Henry found us. He kindly tended to our wounds and our grief, burying my father with gentle words. He then took us the rest of the way to Harrisonburg, returning a week later with our remaining possessions. We never saw him again.

My sobs had slowed to a trickle of tears. I wiped my eyes and returned to bed where I slept fitfully the rest of the night.

20
HOPE

In the morning, the bed I usually shared with Mary was rumpled as if it had been slept in, but Aunt Lydia was no longer there. Mary and I went downstairs.

Mama's eyes appeared red and puffy as she silently prepared breakfast with Aunt Lydia.

"Where is Papa?" whispered Mary.

"I do not know," Mama replied tersely.

A knock sounded at the front door.

I looked at the others, who appeared as puzzled as I was. Uncle Jacob wouldn't knock. Who would be calling this early in the morning?

Mama smoothed back her hair as she walked through the parlor and opened the door.

"Brother Troyer, what brings you here?" she asked. "Please come in."

The reverend followed her to the kitchen and took off his hat as the boys came down the stairs.

"How is the baby?" Brother Troyer asked.

Mama looked startled. "How do you know about Joshua?"

"Jacob is at my house."

Mama closed her eyes and sighed in relief.

"He is a broken man, Elizabeth. I have never known a man so grieved by his own sin," Brother Troyer said. "He would like to come home but is ashamed."

Mama turned toward the window and gazed out at the cold, winter landscape for a long moment. "Please tell him I want him to come home."

Brother Troyer nodded, donned his hat, and left. Through the parlor window, I watched him ride away on his horse.

Other than the bandage covering his left temple, Joshua breathed, slept, and ate normally.

After breakfast, I walked Aunt Lydia home. When I returned to the house, two men on horses were on the road, heading our way. I could tell, even at a distance, they were Uncle Jacob and Brother Troyer.

"He's coming down the road," I announced after I went inside. "Brother Troyer is with him."

"Children, go upstairs," instructed Mama. The children obeyed, solemn and anxious.

I picked up Magdalena who cried and struggled in protest.

Upstairs we gathered in the girls' room, taking comfort from being together. Mary distracted Magdalena with a game of Cat's Cradle. I positioned the bright yellow yarn on Magdalena's tiny fingers while Leon and Amos watched. Peter stared out the window, brooding. Low voices drifted through the floorboards as we waited for the call to come downstairs, uncertain of what to expect once we did.

After nearly thirty tense minutes passed, Mama called us. One by one, we entered the kitchen.

Uncle Jacob, eyes rimmed red, held Joshua at the kitchen table next to Brother Troyer. Mama sat on Uncle Jacob's other side. She appeared exhausted but smiled weakly as we entered and took our seats at the table. Brother Troyer stood to relinquish his seat to Mary and placed his hand on Uncle Jacob's shoulder.

When we were all settled, Uncle Jacob cleared his throat nervously. "Children, I have returned to ask your forgiveness. I have let bitterness and anger change me into a man I do not want to be.

I have been blinded by loss...Rachel...my brother... I have blamed God." He swallowed hard. "And in this rage, I nearly – " His voice faltered before he continued in almost a whisper, "I nearly killed Joshua."

Tears pricked my eyes. I fought to keep them at bay.

"But my loss was also your loss. We all grieve. It is not my right to wallow in my rage and self-pity. I need to be the husband and father you need me to be – like John was. It is what he would want. Rachel, too. But most importantly, it is what the Lord wants from me."

At the mention of my father's name, tears escaped down my cheeks. I brushed them away only to feel new ones take their place.

"I have asked Brother Troyer to help me. He will pray with me and counsel me, and I have vowed to be honest with him as I learn to control my anger and lead this family with love and grace. I want no secrets in this house. If I stumble, you may tell Brother Troyer or others in the church. That way, if I want to avoid being the subject of quilting-circle gossip, I need to practice self-control."

I was relieved. This didn't sound like a hollow promise to change but a real plan, a sincere commitment.

"So I ask you…will you forgive me?" he pled humbly, looking at each of us.

Mary leaned across the corner of the table and hugged her father, a muffled sob escaping from her throat.

I rose and walked toward my uncle with slow steps, not sure what I would do once I reached him. The urge to hit him, to hurt him the way he hurt Joshua, struggled with a desire to believe he meant what he said.

Before I could speak, he rose and wrapped one arm around me, still holding Joshua in the other. "I am sorry," he whispered.

Surprised by this first touch from my uncle, I hesitated, sorting through my warring emotions. Hope won. "I forgive you," I replied.

Leon and Amos stood behind me. He embraced them each in turn as they, too, offered their forgiveness.

A light touch gripped my elbow. I turned to see Mary, tears streaming. As we hugged each other, I felt like a sparrow that had just shaken itself awake after falling.

At that moment, Peter pushed back his chair with a raucous scrape and stood, his face hard. Briefly locking eyes with his father, he turned abruptly and went out the back door.

21
TESTING

DELICIOUS AROMAS OF BAKING BREAD AND OF pumpkin and cinnamon filled the kitchen. Mama had been awake well before the sun came up to start the bread dough rising. The pies Mary and I baked later in the morning sat cooling on dish towels on the kitchen table.

Mama rested in a rocker near the fire, nursing Joshua. Her eyes were closed. Magdalena sat at her feet, prattling to her rag doll.

The rhythmic sound of chopping wood rang from the backyard through the kitchen wall. I looked out the window. Peter chopped, and Amos carried the wood to the woodshed to dry. Drizzly rain dripped off their hats.

"Shouldn't they be coming in to dress now?" I asked.

Christmas was not until next week, but Grandma Clara and Aunt Ann had invited a new church family with no nearby relatives to spend Christmas Day with them, and there was not room for all of us at the table. Instead, we would have an early celebration with Grandma Clara and Aunt Ann this afternoon.

Mary opened the back door and called out. "You need to come in and change your clothes. We have to leave soon. Where are Papa and Leon?"

"In the barn," Peter hollered back.

"Tell Amos to fetch them." Mary shut the door.

Mama opened her eyes. "Thank you, Mary." She lifted Joshua to her shoulder and patted his back to burp him.

A few minutes later, Amos came in, having first removed his dirty boots on the porch. He was out of breath from his run to the barn and back. His cheeks were pink from the cold. He hung his coat and hat on pegs protruding from the wall and padded over to the washbasin Mama had set out. After washing his hands, he headed upstairs. His damp stockings left a trail of wet footprints behind him.

"Change your pants and put on your green shirt," Mama called after him.

Peter came in next and stood in front of the fire to warm his hands after washing them. "It smells good in here," he said.

Uncle Jacob and Leon entered next. "Peter," Uncle Jacob said, "you left the axe in the rain. It will rust if you leave it out."

Peter turned to him with a sullen look. "I've already washed."

Uncle Jacob's jaw clenched as he stared back at Peter.

Leon fled upstairs, his fingertips dripping water from the washbasin.

My stomach tightened. Peter had been deliberately defiant ever since Joshua's injury. Uncle Jacob glowered at him. I glanced at Mama. She was bent over Joshua, settling him in his crib.

"Please go outside, wipe down the axe, and put it away in the woodshed. If it rusts, you will work until you can pay for a replacement. Do you understand?" His voice was stern but controlled.

Peter scowled at him, a determined set in his jaw. Then he stomped out the back door, slamming it behind him.

Uncle Jacob opened the door. "Try that again with less force."

Peter came back in and shot his father a dark look. He spoke with calculated malice as he gestured toward Joshua in his crib. "I learned how to shut doors from you."

Uncle Jacob recoiled from the sting of his words. Mama's face blanched.

Mary sucked in her breath. "Peter!" she scolded.

Uncle Jacob hesitated, then spoke with deliberate composure. "I suppose I deserved that. You will never again witness me slamming doors in anger. Even so, the axe will rust in the rain. I ask you once more to wipe it down and put it away. I will not ask again."

Peter glared at him before stepping out and shutting the door with exaggerated gentleness.

Uncle Jacob ran his hands through his hair, releasing a ragged sigh. He sat heavily in a chair at the table. "He did not close the gate yesterday. If I had not discovered it before the cows, they would have escaped."

"He is testing you, Jacob," Mama said.

"Am I passing?"

"*Ja.* It will take time, but you are doing well." She bent down and kissed his forehead.

Rain drummed the cover on our wagon as we pulled away from the house. I turned around to peek at Aunt Lydia's barn. A tremor of guilt snaked through me. Two months had passed since I discovered her secret activities with runaway slaves. No one ever found out what I'd done. I hadn't even told Peter. I understood now why Uncle Jacob had ordered us to stay off her property. The less we knew, the safer we were.

I asked God's forgiveness for disobeying Uncle Jacob again and again. Still, shame nagged at me for not confessing my transgression to Uncle Jacob himself and even to Aunt Lydia. I thought I could ignore it, but every time I saw Aunt Lydia or even the barn, my guilt stared back at me. I would have to get used to it. Living with Uncle Jacob had become so much better since he'd learned to control his temper. If I upset him, I risked ruining everything. I turned around and faced forward as the wagon lumbered toward town.

"Before we ask the blessing, each one of us should share something we are grateful for from this past year," Grandma Clara said as we sat around the table laden with ham, potatoes, creamed peas and carrots, bread, and pies. "I'll go first. I am grateful for the good harvest we had. Now you say something, Ann."

"Pshaw. Why should I? It is not Thanksgiving."

"Do not be *grexy*, Ann. Surely you are grateful for something." Grandma Clara patted her hand.

Aunt Ann frowned. "I am grateful for peace and quiet in the evening time."

I interpreted that as a not-so-subtle message not to overstay our visit after supper.

Mama was grateful for her children, Mary for her friends, Amos for snow, Leon for the creek behind our house, and Magdalena for her doll.

Next it was Peter's turn. He had been quiet and sullen all day. He turned and met his father's gaze. "I'm grateful Joshua is alive and well."

Uncle Jacob set his mouth in a grim line. "As am I. And I am most grateful for God's grace and mercy."

Color rose in Peter's cheeks, and he looked at his plate.

I was last. "I am grateful for God's care...and for my family."

I caught Grandma Clara's eye. She smiled and winked at me.

Lying in bed that night, I smiled into the darkness and whispered to Mary. "Today turned out to be a good day."

"Any day with pumpkin pie is a good day," she answered.

I chuckled and turned on my side.

She sighed. "I wish Peter would give Papa another chance. How long do you think he can continue like this before Papa explodes again?"

"Maybe today was the end of it. After today Peter must see how hard your papa is trying."

Little did I know of the test yet to come and the role I would play in it.

22
Taking a Chance

The sound of urgent pounding startled me out of my sleep on Christmas Eve. Bolting upright, I whispered, "What was that?"

"Hmmm?" murmured Mary, not quite awake.

I slid out of bed and hurried silently down the stairs. At the bottom, I peeked around the corner into the kitchen as Uncle Jacob, standing at the back door, called out, "Who is it?"

The pounding stopped. "It's me, Skip, your neighbor," was the muffled reply.

"Good heavens, it is one o'clock in the morning." Mama stood in her bedroom doorway in a white cotton nightgown, hastily slipping on a blue dressing robe.

Uncle Jacob opened the door. Skip burst in, red-faced and stammering, "Liddy fell down! She is hurt. Liddy fell down. *She fell down*! We have to get ready. *They are coming.*"

He was so agitated it took a moment for Uncle Jacob to calm him enough to listen. Finally, Uncle Jacob said, "I will come help, Skip. Is she awake or is she asleep?"

"Awake, but she cannot stand up. The passengers are coming. We have to get ready," Skip insisted.

"Passengers? I'm *befuddled*. What are you talking about, Skip? What passengers?" asked Uncle Jacob patiently, pulling on his boots.

I froze for a moment but then dashed upstairs on tiptoe, passing Peter at the bottom of the stairwell. I peeked out the bedroom window toward the Swartzendruber barn. A lantern flickered in the barn loft's window as confirmation. I heard Uncle Jacob downstairs, still trying to make sense of Skip's insistence on getting ready for the "passengers." I rushed back down the stairs.

"I know what he's talking about," I blurted. I hoped I wouldn't have to explain how I knew.

Uncle Jacob and Mama looked at me, bewildered.

"It's-it's runaway slaves. Aunt Lydia helps them. There's a light in her barn window. That's when they come."

Uncle Jacob glared. "Keep your voice down."

I shuddered.

Mama's mouth dropped open, her eyebrows raised in surprise. "How on earth do you know about – ?"

"Never mind that now," Uncle Jacob said gruffly. "She can explain later. I need to see about Lydia."

"Can-can I help?" I asked.

"No," Uncle Jacob and Mama answered simultaneously.

"They'll be hungry. I can cook and bring food to them." My voice quavered.

"We need to get ready. Liddy fell down. She needs help," Skip pulled on Uncle Jacob's arm. His voice rose. "*Schnell!*"

"Quiet, Skip. You'll wake the children," Uncle Jacob warned.

Uncle Jacob and Mama looked at each other. "She is right," Mama said. "Lydia needs help with the cooking. Joshua should wake soon. After he nurses, I will come."

"This is a dangerous business, Elizabeth. Think of the consequences." Uncle Jacob looked at her intently, his voice grave.

"We have no choice," she answered.

"I want to help, too," Peter said from a dark corner.

Uncle Jacob and Mama looked at each other, surprised. Peter had not spoken to his father since Joshua had been hurt, except to answer his questions with as few words as possible.

Mama turned back to Peter. "Who else is awake?"

"No one," Peter said.

"How do you know about this, Peter?" Mama asked.

"I didn't. I heard the knocking and came downstairs and heard you talking," Peter explained.

"You mean you were eavesdropping." Anger flashed across Uncle Jacob's features.

"I was at the bottom of the stairs when you opened the door," Peter said evenly, glowering at his father. "You didn't notice me."

"*Shnell*! We have to hurry," Skip whispered. He pulled Uncle Jacob toward the door.

Uncle Jacob ran a hand through his hair. He winced, sighing heavily. "It is too dangerous. I cannot risk it. If anyone were to see you from the road…"

"I'll go out the back door and hide behind the trees," Peter said.

"I said *no*. Do not argue." Uncle Jacob donned his hat and coat and followed Skip out.

"Go back to bed, children." Mama put her hands on our shoulders and guided us to the stairs.

As Peter and I headed up, Mama returned toward her bedroom and shut her door.

"What do you think they're like?" Peter whispered.

"The runaway slaves?" I asked. "They're nice."

"How would you know?"

I told him about my clandestine visit to Aunt Lydia's barn two months before.

As he listened, Peter's mouth dropped open. "I'm going." He had a determined set in his chin.

"No! Your father said it's too dangerous."

"What's he going to do? Beat me?" Peter sneered. "Do you think I'm afraid of that?"

"He hasn't beaten you in months. Besides, he promised to change."

"That means nothing. It is only a matter of time before he starts in on me again," Peter said, anger flashing in his eyes. "May as well be tonight."

"Well, then I'm coming with you."

Minutes later, Peter and I stepped out into the moonlight shining on the snow-covered backyard and the roof of the summer kitchen, which was closed for the winter. Fat, white flakes drifted down, clinging to our hair as we listened for sounds coming from the road. All was silent except our boots crunching on the snow beneath us.

When we reached our neighbors' door, Peter knocked lightly. Skip opened it. The savory aroma of roast chicken seasoned with garlic and pepper greeted us. Uncle Jacob was helping Aunt Lydia settle on a kitchen chair, her left leg stretched before her on another chair, and her swollen ankle raised on a pillow.

"*Ach*, I will be fine. Really, there is no need for such a fuss, Jacob," Aunt Lydia protested. "Skip should not have come for you. I am only a *doplich* old woman, tripping over my own two feet. I can manage."

"We know *passengers* are due tonight, Lydia," Uncle Jacob said quietly.

"I do not know what you mean by passengers, Jacob. I am not expecting company." Aunt Lydia's voice was calm, but worry flickered in her eyes.

"Skip told us," Uncle Jacob explained.

Aunt Lydia waved her hand dismissively. "You cannot listen to Skip. He is simple."

"But the light in the barn window," I blurted. "Doesn't that mean they are coming?"

Uncle Jacob whirled around and glared at Peter and me, his eyes snapping with sudden fury.

"I told you to stay at home," he snarled.

Aunt Lydia also noticed Peter and me for the first time and looked distressed. "Oh dear. *Gott im himmel*, have mercy. But how – ?"

"We are here to help," Peter said, cutting off her question.

"Go home," ordered Uncle Jacob. "Both of you."

"And risk being seen from the road?" asked Peter sarcastically.

Uncle Jacob stared at us, anger and indecision playing across his face. Finally, his shoulders sagged. "We will discuss this later. Now that you're here, you may as well make yourselves useful."

"Jacob, I could never ask that of you. If the church finds out – You see how I am treated." Aunt Lydia accented her words by chopping the air with agitated hands as she spoke.

"You should have thought of that before you became involved in the first place. The church warned you – "

"I had to do what I knew to be right in my heart."

"It is against the law."

"God's law is higher than the laws of the world."

Uncle Jacob opened his mouth as if to speak but closed it again and shook his head.

"But the children…you must go home now." Aunt Lydia lowered her leg and tried to stand. Wincing in pain, she fell back into the chair.

"We insist. Only this one time," Uncle Jacob replied. "They are on their way. We cannot prevent it now, so we must prepare for them."

"*Outen* the lantern in the barn window. That is the signal. If they do not see it, they will not stop," Aunt Lydia said.

"Then what will they do?" I asked.

"I-I do not know. I suppose they would hide in the woods for now," Aunt Lydia answered.

"But it is snowing. It is too *kalt*. And what would they eat?" I persisted.

"It is settled, Lydia. We are here to help tonight. You can trust us. You saved our Joshua's life. Now let us help you in kind. Tell us what needs to be done," Uncle Jacob said.

"Well, so be it," she conceded. "*Gott segen eich*. The chicken should be done soon. The potatoes and carrots need to be boiled yet. They are in the cellar. Someone can fetch those. I expect no more than five or six passengers, but they will be hungry, so let's boil twelve of each. Bring up two of the big jars of applesauce while you're at it."

For the next half hour, we kept busy. Aunt Lydia, Peter, and I peeled vegetables. While I boiled and seasoned them according to Aunt Lydia's instructions, Peter and Uncle Jacob carried large pails of hot water to fill the washbasin behind the barn.

Soon Mama arrived, bringing apple cobbler ready to bake. Her eyes widened in surprise when she saw Peter and me. "What on earth are you two doing here?"

"We will talk about it later, Elizabeth," Uncle Jacob said. "We have much to do now."

"I had to wake Mary to look after the baby because Susanna was not in her bed. I was afraid she had come here, but I did not expect to see Peter with her."

"What did you tell Mary?" asked Uncle Jacob.

"The truth, of course. She already knows what Lydia does here, does she not?"

"*Ja*, but you should have only told her Lydia fell and needs help. She did not need to know runaways are here tonight. The fewer of us who know, the safer we are."

"Forgive me. I was not thinking."

"Well, what is done is done." Uncle Jacob took the cobbler from her and handed it to me to put in the oven.

While we worked, Aunt Lydia shared the secret password and other important details about the hours to come.

Despite the mundane tasks, I shivered with nervous anticipation. "And are the dishes in the feed bag already?" I asked as she spooned the vegetables into a hot Dutch oven to keep warm.

Silence greeted me. I glanced up to see surprise on the faces of the others.

"How do you know about that, Susanna?" asked Aunt Lydia, concern replacing her surprise. "Who else knows?"

"No one," I answered quickly. My cheeks grew hot, and I looked down, ashamed. "I first noticed the wagon last spring. Every time there was a light in your barn window, it would come during the night. I-I was curious. One night a couple of months ago, I snuck into the barn, and I watched. I-I'm sorry, Aunt Lydia." I turned to Uncle Jacob and Mama and whispered, "I'm sorry."

The adults responded with stunned silence. After a moment, Uncle Jacob spoke, his voice straining to remain in control. "You directly disobeyed my orders to stay off this property, Susanna."

"I know. I'm sorry. I know you have to punish me." I covered my face with my hands as tears of remorse coupled with relief pushed their way to the surface.

"*Ach*. There is no time for this now," Uncle Jacob replied. "We will talk of punishment later."

Through my tears, I noticed Peter's intense observation of his father. My transgression was much greater and more defiant than all of Peter's "tests," and his interest in his father's reaction was evident. Uncle Jacob glanced at him, fully aware of Peter's scrutiny.

A gentle rap sounded on the back door, jerking me out of my thoughts. I wiped my tears on my sleeve.

"That is the conductor. Remember to listen for the password," instructed Aunt Lydia.

23
THE PASSENGERS

"Who is visiting at this hour?" Uncle Jacob called through the door. Silence greeted him for a moment.

"He does not recognize your voice," Aunt Lydia said.

"Lydia hurt herself. I am here to help," Uncle Jacob explained through the door. "Who is visiting at this hour?"

"It is all right, Albert," Aunt Lydia called.

"A friend with friends," a man's voice answered, replying with the password.

Uncle Jacob opened the door. A tall, thin man wearing a brown felt hat and black overcoat stepped inside. His face was lined and red from the cold. A bushy black beard and mustache covered the lower half of his face.

Uncle Jacob extended his hand. "I am Jacob, Lydia's neighbor. She twisted her ankle tonight. My family is here to help."

"Albert." The man took Uncle Jacob's hand and shook it. He removed his hat and nodded at Mama. "Ma'am," he said politely. He looked nervously at Aunt Lydia.

"It is all right, Albert. They discovered our work and want to help tonight. They can be trusted," assured Aunt Lydia.

"How can you be certain?" Albert appeared tense, ready to run out the door.

Aunt Lydia looked at Uncle Jacob for a long moment.

"I've known Jacob since he was born," she said quietly. "In recent years I've known him as a cold, bitter man."

Anger flashed across Uncle Jacob's face, and he opened his mouth to speak. Before he could utter a word, Aunt Lydia continued. "But that is not who he *really* is. That is only a mask for his grief. The man underneath that anger is good and kind, and above all, he is trustworthy."

Uncle Jacob closed his mouth. His face reddened, but he no longer looked angry.

Albert looked at him in silence, weighing Aunt Lydia's words.

"May God bless you for your service tonight," Albert said. "Is everything ready to go?"

"*Ja*, it is right here." Uncle Jacob lifted the large basket of food.

"Can I help?" I asked. "I know where things are...what to do."

Uncle Jacob hesitated.

"She may as well, Jacob. I will stay here and wash the pots and pans before going home," Mama said.

Uncle Jacob looked at Peter. "Son, I want you to head on home. Take care no one sees you, and do not say anything about this to Leon, Amos, or even Magdalena."

Peter frowned and opened his mouth as if to argue. Then he huffed out his breath, turned away, and trudged outside.

"All right, then. Let's go." Uncle Jacob followed Albert out the back door. I trailed behind.

We greeted four weary travelers in the barn: a young man, a woman who appeared to be in her thirties, a girl who looked close to my age, and a younger boy, about six years old.

I looked at the boy curiously.

His skin was much lighter than that of the others. His hair, curled tightly, had a warm golden tint. A second man, older than the first, emerged through the loose board at the back of the barn, bringing the total to five.

Albert was already unloading the straw in the back of the wagon with a pitchfork.

Remembering to include Albert, I removed six plates, cups, knives, and forks from the feed bag and shyly distributed them to the hungry travelers. Once the wagon was cleared, I helped Uncle Jacob place the food along its edge on the back.

While they ate, I read the instructions Aunt Lydia had dictated to me while waiting for the vegetables to cook. The paper trembled in my hands. "Do you have any questions?" I concluded.

They shook their heads.

Grabbing a handful of straw, I smudged away the charcoal words until they could no longer be seen. Aunt Lydia had been nervous to have the incriminating words written down until Mama had suggested using Skip's drawing charcoal and smudging them away.

Albert removed a knife from his pocket and opened it.

"May I?" I held out my hand.

Albert looked surprised but handed me the knife. I walked to the back of the barn and found the support beam covered in notches. I carefully added five notches, aware of Uncle Jacob watching silently behind me.

"Lydia has helped a lot of people," he said quietly.

I nodded.

After saying goodnight to the guests, Albert left in his wagon. Uncle Jacob and I returned home after washing the used dishes.

I opened the back door. The smell of pine boughs greeted me. A row of woolen stockings dangled from the fireplace mantle. Mama was still awake. "Merry Christmas," she whispered. "I had almost forgotten."

"Merry Christmas," I answered, trudging upstairs to my bed.

I woke early the next morning, despite having been up so late. Mary and Magdalena were nowhere in sight. I must have slept through when they woke and dressed for the day.

The smell of frying bacon was irresistible. Magdalena shrieked with delight downstairs.

Dressing quickly, I remembered the runaways in the barn next door and wondered if they were awake yet.

The boys' bedroom door was open. I peeked in and found it empty.

"Merry Christmas, 'Sanna," Magdalena shouted when she spotted me coming down the stairs.

"Merry Christmas to you." I kneeled to embrace my sister.

"Look what Saint Nicolas gave me." She pointed at a wooden doll cradle. It had stars carved out of the sides, identical to the cradles Uncle Jacob had made for Mary and me when we were small.

"It's beautiful, Maggie. You must have been a good girl this year."

The table was loaded with food – bacon, hotcakes, fried eggs. I spied extra food warming on the stovetop.

"We need to eat quickly, children," Mama said. "Aunt Lydia hurt herself last night, so we need to take breakfast to her and Skip as well." She gave me a pointed look. I understood. The younger children were not to know who else we fed that morning and in the days to come.

After breakfast, Uncle Jacob handed each child a stocking from the fireplace mantle. Inside, we found hard candy from the store, a rare treat given only at Christmas.

I popped a peppermint in my mouth, savoring its sweetness melting on my tongue. I tucked the rest into my apron pocket.

Uncle Jacob placed in front of me a gift wrapped in plain brown paper and tied with string. "Merry Christmas."

I looked at him, surprised. I tore the paper off and found a beautiful wooden box. Uncle Jacob had carved delicate roses on its sides and lid. "It is beautiful," I whispered. "*Danke.*"

"Don't thank me. Thank Saint Nicolas." He looked pointedly at Magdalena and winked.

I smiled.

Mary was given a similar box. Amos delighted in a new wooden steam engine. Peter and Leon opened and admired their shiny pocketknives.

"*Danke*, Papa," Peter said.

"You're welcome, son." Uncle Jacob put his hand on Peter's shoulder. Peter stiffened but did not move away.

Next we received new clothes. Mary, Magdalena, and I reveled in our new matching blue dresses and crisp white linen aprons.

Magdalena immediately donned her apron, especially pleased because it was her first.

"Susanna, will you help me take this food to Lydia?" Uncle Jacob lifted the basket Mama had filled.

"Of course."

After leaving some of the food with Skip and Aunt Lydia, we entered the barn. The men were waiting downstairs. One was tall and young, perhaps in his early twenties. The other was shorter and older with graying hair, very dark skin, and bowed legs. One of his front teeth was missing.

I wondered about their relationship with the woman who obviously was the children's mother. I heard her and the children's quiet murmurs behind the barn as they washed.

"Merry Christmas," Uncle Jacob greeted them.

"Merry Christmas," the men answered.

Uncle Jacob cleared a space on the barn floor, and I helped him unload the food and breakfast dishes.

The woman and children climbed through the loose board and joined us. The woman and girl had wrapped their hair in brightly-colored fabric. Other than the obvious age difference, they almost could have been twins. Both had smooth, molasses-colored skin and dark eyes fringed with thick lashes. They smiled with even white teeth and dimpled cheeks.

As the group ate, I collected their dirty clothes from the barrel they had placed them in the night before according to my instructions. I loaded them in an empty feed bag, holding my breath against the smell of bodies unwashed for weeks trapped in their fibers. I dragged the bag of clothes behind the barn as Aunt Lydia had requested.

The girl appeared through the loose board, followed by the boy, his face smeared with maple syrup.

I smiled shyly. "Merry Christmas."

The girl smiled back. "Thank you. As long as we're away from the Big House, it's merry."

She and the boy walked to the washbasin. He smiled at me timidly.

"What is the Big House?" I asked.

"Master's house down on the plantation," explained the girl. She watched the boy splash his face with water from the basin.

"When did you escape?"

"Ten days ago. We're heading north to Canada. Slavery is outlawed there, and we can live free." She handed soap to the boy.

The boy finished washing and climbed back into the barn.

"How do you know which way to go?"

"We follow the North Star at night. Also the conductors and stationmasters give us directions."

"What if you can't see the stars? What if it's a cloudy night?"

"It don't always work, but when we're in the woods, sometimes we know which way to go by how the moss grows on the trees. It usually only grows on the north side."

I imagined stumbling through the cold, dark woods at night, running my hands along the trees for direction, wild animals' eyes glowing from the gloom as they watched. I shuddered.

"Has it been horrible? The trip I mean?"

"Better than stayin' there."

"Was that boy your brother?"

"Yes. He's Lewis. And my mama is Dinah."

"What about your papa?"

"Don't have a papa. He was sold before I was born, along with my older brother James. Mama ain't seen them since."

"Are you going to try to find them?"

"How? We don't know where they went."

"How old was your older brother when he was sold?"

"Only four. Mama never got over it."

I shook my head in misery at the thought of one of my siblings being ripped from our family. My heart grew heavy.

"My papa died over a year ago. That man in there is my uncle Jacob. He married my mother." I thought for a moment. "Is one of those men in there your brother's papa?"

The girl snorted with derision. "George and Virgil? No. We escaped from my brother's papa."

"But…" I began.

"He's the master we ran from," explained the girl patiently.

"Oh," I said, confused. Remembering the boy's light skin, shock replaced confusion. "Oh," I repeated, embarrassed.

"He *forced* her." The girl's cheeks reddened. "When he started to look at me like he looked at Mama, we ran away."

"I'm sorry," I whispered. My throat tightened. "I didn't realize…I didn't know. Oh, how awful."

"It's over now." She gently touched my arm. "What's your name?"

"Susanna," I sniffled.

"I'm Alice."

"Nice to meet you, Alice," I said, composing myself. I reached into my pocket for a handkerchief and felt the lumpy Christmas stocking. "I have a Christmas gift for you and your brother. Do you like candy?"

24
Four Months

THE NEXT DAY WAS MONDAY, BUT WE DIDN'T HAVE to go to school. In fact, we had more than a week off after Christmas. On Wednesday, I was going to spend the day with Martha at her house. Mama said I could even sleep there for the night. I had not had the chance to visit with a girl my own age since I left Pennsylvania, and I was thirsty for companionship. The brief conversations Martha and I had after church or during school lunch didn't count. Those times were too short, and we were frequently interrupted.

Then on Friday evening, the youth of the church planned to hold a frolic at the schoolhouse. It was to be the first party I'd enjoy since moving to Virginia. We were going to build snowmen, go on a sleigh ride, and play blind man's bluff outside. Then come in for hot cider and potato doughnuts. Afterward, we were going to have a taffy pull. I'd been drooling over the thought of that sweet, gooey taffy for days.

After breakfast that morning, Uncle Jacob and Mama asked to speak to me alone in their bedroom. My heart dropped. I had hoped they decided not to punish me for sneaking into Aunt Lydia's barn. I even thought they might have forgotten.

I meekly followed Mama into the room where Uncle Jacob waited. His face was stern. "How long have you been sneaking into Lydia's barn?"

I looked at the floor. "I only did it once."

"Look at me when I speak to you."

I raised my head. Tears welled in my eyes. "Only once. Last October."

"Why did you do such a thing?" Mama asked.

"I-I was curious. The light in the barn window – it meant something. I needed to know what it was for. I'm sorry. But isn't it a good thing that I knew they were coming?"

Mama took my hand. "God can redeem even our mistakes, but do not use that to justify disobedience."

"I know what I did was wrong. I'm sorry." I looked up at Uncle Jacob, and my voice trembled. "Are you going to punish me?"

"Your mother and I decided a fitting punishment for sneaking out is to keep you in for a while."

"Keep me in?" I was confused.

"You will stay home this week. No visits with Martha, and no frolic." Mama's face was stern.

My heart caught, and I pulled my hand away from hers. "What? No, Mama! Can't I muck out the horse stalls or something instead? I'll clean the chicken coop again."

"No. This is what we have decided," Uncle Jacob said.

"What you did was very serious, Susanna," Mama said. "You not only disobeyed us, but you also trespassed on Aunt Lydia's property. That was a betrayal of trust."

"But I'm sorry." My lip quivered. I bit it to hold back angry tears. I breathed heavily through my nose. This was so unfair.

"Be that as it may, you will stay in this week." Mama's voice was firm. "You may go to your room to compose yourself, but then I expect you to come downstairs to help take breakfast to Aunt

Lydia's. It is getting late, and her visitors will be hungry."

"*Ja*, Mama." I slipped out the door and dashed upstairs before Mary could see my stricken face.

No frolic? I had looked forward to this frolic more than anything. My heart sank at the thought of all the fun that was still going to happen without me. I buried my face in my pillow and wept.

After my tears had dried, I followed Uncle Jacob to Aunt Lydia's. He carried an apple crate filled with muffins, smoked sausages, and canned cherries. I lagged several paces behind, still stinging from disappointment. What I did was wrong, but a knot of resentment twisted inside me at the sight of him.

Uncle Jacob knocked on Aunt Lydia's side door that led to her kitchen. Skip greeted us. "Hi. Liddy's hurt. She fell down."

"*Ja*, I remember that," Uncle Jacob said. "Where is she?"

"I am back here, Jacob." Aunt Lydia's voice came from the parlor.

"Whatcha got in there?" Skip asked, peering into the crate.

"Breakfast for the passengers." Uncle Jacob reached into the crate and pulled out a muffin.

"And it looks like we have something here for you."

Skip beamed. "*Danke*," he said, reaching for the muffin.

We found Aunt Lydia on the sofa with her discolored foot propped up on a pillow. Her face lit up when she saw the apple crate full of food. "Oh, bless you. You can take it into the barn now. Be sure to look around first to make certain no one watches from the road."

She looked at me. "Susanna. How nice of you to help your papa."

I winced, but I didn't correct her. I forced a smile and nodded.

We walked back into the kitchen. Uncle Jacob set the crate on the table. "Wait here a minute. I want to take a look around outside first." He left through the side door.

After a moment, he returned. "No one in sight." He picked up the crate and looked at me solemnly. "Are you certain you still want to do this? If you want to go home, I can manage alone."

I nodded and followed him to the barn.

Inside, dusty light filtered through the cracks and upper window. All was quiet except for a faint sound of splashing coming from behind the barn.

"Breakfast!" I called softly.

Rustling sounds floated down from the loft as bodies squeezed through openings in the hay bale wall. Alice's feet appeared at the top of the ladder, followed by the rest of her as she climbed down. Lewis and their mother descended after her. George brought up the rear. They gathered around as Uncle Jacob pulled muffins out of the crate. I set out clean dishes from the feed bag where Mama and I had placed them the night before.

The splashing sounds stopped, and Virgil appeared through the loose board in the back, his face and bare upper torso dripping with water. When he saw us, he stopped short. "'Scuse me. I'll get the rest of my clothes on." He walked quickly to the ladder and climbed up. His back was crisscrossed with angry purple scars, healed over cuts from whips. They looked like the tangled stems of a bramble bush.

I swallowed hard and looked away. No one else seemed to notice. Uncle Jacob had his back turned, still unloading the crate. The others had probably all seen his scars before. Maybe they had some of their own.

My punishment did not seem as harsh now. Two months ago if Uncle Jacob discovered me sneaking to Aunt Lydia's, my back may have resembled Virgil's. I shuddered.

Uncle Jacob walked over to me. "I will wash the dirty clothes and hang them to dry. Lydia needs to stay off her feet today. I want you to stay and help wash the dishes."

"*Ja*, of course," I said. He had willingly taken the less desirable job. Washing dishes was much easier than washing clothes that filthy. He was trying to be kind. I felt my anger toward him draining away.

I settled next to Alice after he left. "When do you leave?"

"Tomorrow after dark."

"Will you write to me when you get to Canada?"

She frowned. "I don't know my letters yet. I'm gonna learn, though."

"If you stayed longer, I could teach you."

She shook her head. "It's not safe to stay too long in one place. We've got to keep moving."

"I know! I'll teach you my address. You memorize it and then have someone else write to me. I want to know you got there safe and sound."

Alice spent the next few minutes practicing my address. It didn't take long before she could repeat it back to me perfectly.

"You got it!" I said. "Say it every night before you go to sleep. That way you won't forget. Now how long do you think it will take to get to Canada?"

"Virgil says maybe four months more."

My jaw dropped. "*Four months?*"

She nodded. "Four months if we move fast. Virgil says he didn't want to take us because Lewis would slow us down. Then George asked to come. He's so old Virgil nearly gave up the idea of going at all, but Mama kept after him. Then he heard Master's gonna sell him to a cousin in South Carolina, and he knew if he was ever gonna escape, he had to go now."

"Why didn't he go on his own? Why did he agree to take the rest of you with him?"

"Mama's been like a mama to him most of his life. She's the closest thing he's got. She didn't like the way Master was looking at me. In the end, he couldn't say no to her."

Four months of hiding in wagons and barns, cellars and attics. Finding their way through the woods at night by watching the stars and relying on tree moss to point them in the right direction. Four months of being cold, tired, dirty, and hungry. Creeks to cross, hills to climb, the danger of wild animals chasing them, or even worse, the slave catchers themselves. I shuddered.

"I'll pray for you." I didn't know what else to say.

25
A Close Call

ALICE AND HER FAMILY LEFT FOR CANADA THE next day on the Underground Railroad. That's what Aunt Lydia called the network of people who helped runaway slaves find their way to freedom. On this secret "railroad," they were called "passengers" and Aunt Lydia was called a "stationmaster." Albert, the "conductor," was a Quaker, as were many others who ran the Underground Railroad along with free blacks and other escaped slaves. Aunt Lydia had come to know Charlotte, Albert's wife, years ago when Charlotte taught Skip in a school for the simple-minded in a town forty miles away. He had lived there before Aunt Lydia brought him home after their parents died. That was how she became involved as a stationmaster.

The day after Alice and the others left, heavy pounding on our front door interrupted our supper. Uncle Jacob pushed back his chair with a loud scrape, stood, and walked through the parlor toward the door.

From my place at the table, I craned my neck to see the identity of our unexpected guest. Uncle Jacob opened the door. Two men stood outside wearing black hats and overcoats, one tall and dark, the other short and stocky with red hair. With them were two large dogs with tan and black fur and upright, pointed ears.

"Can I help you?" Uncle Jacob asked.

"May we come in?" the shorter man replied.

"What is this about?"

"We're looking for these runaways." The man held up three posters.

Uncle Jacob took them and read them. "I am afraid I cannot help you."

"May we come inside?" asked the tall man, menace in his voice.

Uncle Jacob stepped aside, and they strode through the parlor and into the kitchen where the rest of us sat around the table. Their muddy boots left tracks on the floor, along with the dogs' paw prints. They glanced around the room, barely acknowledging us. The tall man walked into Uncle Jacob and Mama's bedroom.

"Now see here – " said Uncle Jacob, taking a step toward the bedroom.

"No, *you* see here," snapped the shorter man. "We are fugitive slave catchers hired by Mr. Thomas Burton to find his property, and that is exactly what we will do. And you, sir, are mandated by the Fugitive Slave Act to cooperate with us in our endeavor."

The sound of dresser drawers sliding open and slamming shut again came from the bedroom. I clenched my fists. Why would he need to look in places too small to hide a person?

Mama pressed her lips together. Her flared nostrils divulged her barely concealed indignation.

The tall man reentered the kitchen and clomped down the cellar stairs.

"Why do you search my home?" asked Uncle Jacob.

Breaking glass tinkled below us. I scowled. Couldn't he be more careful?

"We have been told of a suspicious wagon headed in this direction a few nights back, and we intend to get some answers. It is our federal duty to search this and all neighboring properties" the short man said.

My pulse raced as I thought of Aunt Lydia. Would they find the dishes in the feed bag? Did the children's clothing still hang on the line to dry behind the barn? That would be hard to explain since no children lived there. Would they find the opening in the hay wall? I faked a disinterested expression to mask my growing fear for Aunt Lydia and for Alice's family. I hoped they were far enough away by now to avoid capture by these vile men.

The tall man returned from the cellar and immediately climbed the stairs to the bedrooms, a dog leading the way.

I pictured him searching through my bedroom, touching my things, and I cringed. He started in the boys' room. His footsteps clomped, and furniture scraped overhead as he shoved it aside.

"Search all you want. You will not find runaway slaves here," said Uncle Jacob with a confidence I did not feel.

"Have you seen a wagon traveling this road in the dead of night?" asked the short man.

"No," responded Uncle Jacob truthfully.

He had not seen the wagon traveling. It had already arrived in Aunt Lydia's barn when he saw it.

"Have you seen suspicious activity or Negroes unknown to you in this area in the past week?"

"No."

Again he spoke the truth. After spending three days with the runaways in Aunt Lydia's barn, he could say he knew them.

Next he asked Mama and Mary the same questions. They also could answer without lying. They had not gone into the barn, so they had not seen the runaways. Peter, like Uncle Jacob, had not seen the wagon and answered honestly.

He turned to me. "Have you seen a wagon traveling this road in the dead of night?"

I gulped. Could he hear my heart pounding? If I said "no," it would be a lie. "I-I've seen wagons from time to time when I have trouble sleeping at night."

Mary sucked in her breath.

"I can't-I can't tell you where they were going, though." That was true. I couldn't tell him.

He turned his attention to Leon and Amos who, of course, knew nothing. Relieved he had no more questions for me, I exhaled and slumped in my chair. The noises overhead continued as the footsteps stomped inside the girls' bedroom. The door of the chiffarobe creaked open. I imagined his fingers pawing through my dresses, my underclothes, the dog's wet nose snuffling through it all. My stomach was queasy with disgust. I would have to wash it all before wearing it again.

Thirty minutes after invading our house, the men and dogs left to search our barn, summer kitchen, and other outbuildings. Aunt Lydia's property would be next.

26
COVER-UP

"We have to warn her," I whispered.

"We cannot risk it," Uncle Jacob answered.

"But – "

"He is right, Susanna. All we can do is pray and wait," Mama said.

I picked up one of the posters lying on the kitchen table where the short man had left it and read: "*One hundred dollar reward for the return of runaway from the subscriber in Hampton Elizabeth City County, on the 28th of November, a negro fellow called George Simpson; he is about 50 years of age, gray hair, legs bowed, low sized, very black complexion, one front tooth missing, and generally smiles when spoken to; by trade a caulker.*"

A chill ran up my spine as I recognized the name and description of one of the men who had hidden in Aunt Lydia's barn with Alice and her family.

I continued reading, "*When he left our plantation, he had on a pair of blue trousers, brown linen shirt, and a nankeen jacket. We purchased him from Mr. James Woolsey, who bought him from a Mr. Richard Munford of Hampton. Masters of vessels, and others, are forewarned carrying off or harboring said Negro, as the utmost rigor of the law will be enforced against such. Mr. Thomas Burton, Norfolk, July 10.*"

The second poster described the younger man, Virgil, also in minute detail. A two hundred dollar reward was offered for his return. Alice's mother, Dinah, was featured on the third poster with Alice and her brother Lewis mentioned almost as afterthoughts. Alice was described as *delicately made* and Lewis as *a bright mulatto*. The reward for their return was three hundred dollars.

My stomach clenched.

Mary took the posters from me to read. "Are these the ones – ?" she began.

"Shh," Mama said, glancing at the younger children. "The dishes need to be cleared." She pushed her chair back abruptly, stood, and grabbed two plates, still half full.

Mary clamped her mouth shut, but she looked at me with a question in her eyes.

I gave her a slight nod, and her face paled.

"Boys, we have chores to do. Get your boots on," Uncle Jacob said.

The boys obeyed and followed him out the back door.

Mary stood and poured steaming water from the pot on the stove into the washbasin. I brought dishes to her and helped dry until enough time had passed for Uncle Jacob and the boys to make it to our barn.

"I need to use the privy." I rushed through the door before Mama could suspect that was only a ruse.

Once outside, I glanced around to make sure the searching men were not in sight and clambered over the fence. I hid behind the woodshed and peeked around the corner. The men must still be in one of the buildings on our property. I dashed to Aunt Lydia's back door, turned the knob, and slipped inside. "Aunt Lydia!"

"Susanna? Is that you?" she called. "I'm in the kitchen."

She sat at the table, stitching a button on a man's shirt. Skip stood at the washbasin, humming as he cleaned their supper dishes.

My message came out in a rush. "Slave hunters are searching our property. They're coming here next."

Alarmed, Aunt Lydia jerked her head up to look at me, set down her mending, and winced as she tried to stand on her sore ankle.

"Will they find anything in the barn? The dishes? What about the wash on the line?" I asked.

Her eyes widened. "*Ach*. They will discover it for certain. I have become too careless."

"I'll take care of it." I rushed out the door before she could stop me and scanned my surroundings. The slave hunters were still not in sight.

I sprinted to the clothesline behind the barn and snatched the children's clothing off of it. The clothes were frozen stiff. Breathing heavily, I looked around wildly. Where could I hide them? The creek gurgled behind me. That might work. A clump of debris, covered in snow, was wedged firmly against the bank in one spot. I plunged my feet through the thin layer of ice clinging to the bank, waded over to the debris, and shoved the clothes underneath. Freezing water filled my shoes as I piled rocks and branches over the clothes. I climbed out of the creek, drenched to the knees, my hem and sleeves dripping. My hands and feet ached with the cold as if pierced by shards of ice.

I lifted the board in the back of the barn and peeked inside. It was empty except for the barn cats. I eased through the opening and ran to the feed bag full of clean dishes waiting for the next passengers to arrive. Fortunately, the straw strewn on the floor masked my wet footprints. A burlap bag of oats rested against the wall along with a large scoop. My hands were so numb and shaky that I couldn't untie the twine holding it closed.

I whirled around to look for something to cut it open. A pair of pruning shears hanging on the wall glinted in the dim light coming through the window. They were just out of reach. I jumped to knock them loose and ducked as they fell toward me, sharp end first. They clattered to the floor. I snatched them up and jabbed them into the burlap. The bag opened. Using the scoop, I poured oats over the dishes.

Men's voices, mingled with Aunt Lydia's, filtered through the wall. I peeked through the crack between the barn doors to see where they were. They were approaching the barn! I picked up the now half-empty bag and poured the remaining oats over the top of the dishes, hoping it was enough to cover them. The voices were louder as they came closer.

The barn door creaked open just as I snuck out through the board in the back.

I didn't have time to go up the ladder to the loft to plug the opening in the hay wall. I could only hope the runaways had thought to do that before they left. I stumbled home on numb feet, praying silently the whole time.

"Where have you been?" Mama demanded when I burst through the back door.

Ignoring her, I hurried upstairs to peek out the bedroom window. Mary followed and hovered behind me. I shivered violently.

"You went to Aunt Lydia's, didn't you?" she whispered.

I nodded, too out of breath to speak.

Aunt Lydia stood with her hands on her hips in front of the barn, its door wide open. Two unfamiliar horses were hitched to the fence.

Mama came upstairs. "Susanna, you're blue. You're all wet. What have you been doing?"

My teeth chattered in response.

"She went to Aunt Lydia's," Mary answered for me.

Mama gasped. "Did they see you?"

I shook my head.

After several minutes, both men and the dogs emerged from the barn and stood talking with

Aunt Lydia. Finally, the men walked toward their horses, and she returned to her home. I released a shuddering breath. If they'd found anything in her barn, they would have taken her with them.

I whispered to Mama and Mary, "They are leaving. I don't think they found anything."

"I pray they did not," Mama said.

"I hid the clothes in the creek and covered the dishes with oats. Unless they discovered the space behind the wall of hay in the loft, they found nothing," I said, trying to reassure myself as much as the others.

I sat on the bed and bent to untie my shoelaces, but my stiff, reddened fingers were useless. I tucked them into my armpits to warm them. Mary knelt in front of me, tugged at my laces until they came loose, and pulled off my soaked shoes and stockings.

Mama brought up a towel and a basin filled with lukewarm water. Mary lifted my feet and placed them in the basin. Then she massaged them under the water, bringing the feeling back. Pain blazed through my extremities as life returned to them. I gasped and squeezed back tears.

The next morning Aunt Lydia rapped lightly on our back door. When Mama saw who it was, she sent Leon and Amos to the woodpile for more kindling.

"Lydia." Mama wrapped her in a hug. "Are you safe?"

"*Ja*, I believe so for now, thanks to Susanna," Aunt Lydia said. "The dogs scented them, but they found nothing. I told them the dogs probably smelled all manner of things, but they would find no runaways in my barn."

"They are suspicious now," Uncle Jacob said. "This is a dangerous business, Lydia."

"*Ja*, I know. That is why I have come. I am truly grateful for your help, but it cannot happen again. I cannot put your family at risk. I will send word to Albert that I must stop for a time."

"But who will take care of the passengers?" I asked.

"There are others," Aunt Lydia said. "I intend to continue my work in time, but I need to stop until those slave catchers find another place to do their hunting."

"That is wise, Lydia. The fine for aiding the escape of a slave is now one thousand dollars. You could even be imprisoned for up to six months if you are caught."

"*Ja*, I know. That's what those men said last night. It's the Fugitive Slave Act, a despicable law. Of course, everything about slavery is loathsome," Aunt Lydia said.

I shuddered at the risk we had taken, but I soon learned that our risk paled in comparison to the danger faced by Alice's family.

27
TRAPPED

THAT AFTERNOON AS I LEFT THE CHICKEN HOUSE with a basket of eggs, I heard the creak of a wagon and glanced up. Horror-stricken, I recognized the faces of the slave hunters who had searched our home. I darted back into the chicken house and peered out a knothole in the wall. What I saw made my stomach lurch.

Shackled in chains, a dark-skinned man sat in the wagon bed, his back, turned toward me, streaked red with blood. He was obviously a runaway who had been caught and whipped.

As the wagon passed, I saw a small body in his arms, bare legs dangling, one of them covered in dark red blood. The child's skin was a lighter shade of brown, and I was startled by a horrible thought. The man lifted his head and turned to look behind him. It was Virgil. The boy he held – Alice's little brother, Lewis, – wasn't moving.

A scream threatened to surface. I clamped my hand over my mouth.

After the wagon passed, I ran inside the house. I slammed the door behind me and stood trembling in the kitchen.

Mama heard me and called from her bedroom, "Leon, is that you slamming the door? What did I tell you about that?"

"No, Mama. It's me." My voice shook.

Mama appeared in the doorway from the bedroom. "Susanna, whatever is the matter?"

"They caught Virgil and Lewis," I cried.

"Lewis? The little boy?"

"*Ja*. I saw them in the slave hunters' wagon. Lewis wasn't moving. I saw blood on him."

"Oh, no." Mama shook her head as if trying to shake away the horror. She wrapped her arms around me.

"What if Lewis is dead?" Tears rolled down my cheeks and dripped from my chin.

"If he is, you know he is in heaven," Mama said. "He is better off there than here."

"But he is only a little boy. How could God let this happen? Doesn't God care for them?

Aren't they worth more than the sparrows?" I asked.

"Of course, he cares for them. He sees what is happening, and his heart breaks over it."

"Then why doesn't he do something to stop it?"

Mama sighed. "I wish I could understand myself. Then I could explain it to you. But I cannot. All I know is that even though man often chooses evil, God is always good. He does care, and all will be made right in the end. We have to believe that. Let us pray for them, Susanna. At least we can do that much."

"We should tell Aunt Lydia."

"I think we should wait until morning. The slave hunters are too close. If they decide to question us again, it would be best if we were not found in Aunt Lydia's company."

That night I lay awake for a long time, unable to stop my thoughts or the images in my head. I grieved for Lewis and his mother the most, knowing they might never see each other again. After finally falling asleep, I dreamed of George and Lewis in the slave hunters' wagon, both dead. Blood streamed from the back of the wagon, splashing onto the dirt road as it passed. I woke crying, unable to sleep again until nearly daybreak.

After Uncle Jacob and the boys left to do chores the next morning, Aunt Lydia knocked on our back door.

"Lydia, please come in," Mama said. "I am afraid we have some bad news."

"Oh, dear. So do I." Aunt Lydia's brow furrowed. "What is yours?"

"Magdalena, please take these things upstairs to your room and put them away." Mama handed Magdalena a pair of newly darned stockings.

"It is about Virgil…and Lewis," Mama said after Magdalena left the room. "Susanna saw they had been captured yesterday."

"That is what I came to tell you. Albert found out what happened from a conductor thirty miles north. Lewis was caught in a trap – " Aunt Lydia began.

I interrupted her. "A trap? What kind of trap?"

"The kind used to catch wild animals, only this one was surely set to capture runaways."

"Is he still alive?" I asked.

"He was when they caught him," Lydia said. "Although his leg was mangled in the trap, so if infection sets in…" She shook her head.

"What about Virgil?" Mary asked. "Was he also caught in a trap?"

"No. He was caught trying to free Lewis. Lewis's screams attracted the slave hunters."

"What about the others?" I asked. "What about Alice?"

"Alice, Dinah, and George all made it across a nearby creek where the conductor waited, and the dogs could no longer track them. They hid in the brush on the other side and watched as Virgil and Lewis were captured."

"Oh, how *greislich* for them," Mama said.

My stomach roiled, and I swallowed hard. "*Ja*, it is horrible." How helpless Dinah and Alice must have felt to hear Lewis's screams and watch him be hauled away. Would they ever see him again?

Aunt Lydia continued. "George and the conductor had to hold Dinah down to keep her from betraying their hiding place. Otherwise, they all would have been caught."

"What will happen to Virgil and Lewis?" I asked.

"Well, they both will be returned to their master. Virgil will likely be punished severely. This was not his first escape attempt."

"And Lewis?" I asked.

"If the boy lives, I do not expect he will undergo any further punishment. He will probably be nursed in the big house until he is well enough to work."

"Will Dinah and Alice ever see him again?" Mary asked.

"Only the Lord knows, Mary," Mama said.

"Isn't there anything we can do?" I asked.

"All we can do for Virgil and Lewis is pray," Aunt Lydia said. "But there will be others to come."

"You agreed yesterday that it is too dangerous," Mama protested. "The dogs smelled their scent on your property, Lydia. They'll come looking again. There's nothing more we can do."

"There is one thing," Aunt Lydia said thoughtfully. "The passengers need costumes to wear for the times they might be seen."

"Costumes?" Mary asked.

"*Ja.* We can disguise them to look like railroad workers, nurses, Quaker women wearing veiled bonnets, riverboat hands, nannies, whatever we can think of," Aunt Lydia explained.

"May we, Aunt Elizabeth?" asked Mary.

Mama frowned. "I guess that is harmless enough, but we had better ask your father."

"Absolutely not." Uncle Jacob sat at the table that evening after supper, his expression unyielding. "We have done enough. It is too dangerous."

"It is only sewing," Mama said in a soothing voice. "Even if those awful men return and find us in a sewing circle, they will not suspect a thing."

Uncle Jacob shook his head gravely. "I do not like it."

"Think on it a while longer before you say no. It seems we must do something to help. I confess I admire Lydia's courage, but I am not asking you to allow us to hide them here." She stood and, leaning down, kissed him on the forehead before picking up the soup kettle to wash.

Uncle Jacob only stared at the floor and frowned, rubbing his chin with his hand. Twenty minutes later, I stole a peek at him before going upstairs to my room. He remained in the same posture, lost in thought.

28
Reconciliation

Uncle Jacob gave permission for us to sew costumes for the Underground Railroad after all, much to our surprise. A sewing circle met in our kitchen every Tuesday evening after supper. Aunt Lydia made arrangements with Albert to retrieve the clothing from a hiding spot each month and distribute them to other "station masters" throughout Virginia and even to states in the North.

Five months later, Grandma Clara visited unexpectedly on a Tuesday evening and discovered us sewing with Aunt Lydia at the kitchen table.

"Why, Lydia, what a surprise," Grandma Clara said.

"Aunt Lydia has invited us to form a sewing circle, Clara," Mama said stiffly.

Grandma Clara picked up the nurse's frock I was stitching together. "Oh? What is this?"

Uncle Jacob cleared his throat and said, "Mother, will you please step into the parlor for a moment?"

She looked at us, puzzled, and followed him through the doorway.

Several uncomfortable minutes passed as the rest of us worked silently.

When Grandma Clara returned to the kitchen, she shocked us all. "I wish to help," she announced, her cheeks red and eyes moist. "I have always believed Lydia is doing right. I have been too much of a coward to stand beside her. Will you forgive me, Lydia?"

"Of course I will, Clara." Aunt Lydia scooted her chair over to make room for another seamstress.

When we finished with our work for the night, Grandma Clara walked Aunt Lydia home.

Hours later, Grandma Clara's wagon wheels crunched as she pulled away from our house.

That Sunday at church, Grandma Clara surprised us even further. When we entered the sanctuary, the men and boys sat on one side, and the women and girls sat on the other as usual. But something was different. Aunt Lydia was not alone in her pew. Grandma Clara sat next to her.

The church members' whispers and stolen glances at the pair indicated that the congregation was unsettled by this turn of events. Wide-eyed and frowning, Aunt Ann appeared particularly unnerved.

I walked down the aisle and stopped next to the pew where Aunt Lydia and Grandma Clara sat holding hands.

I looked back at Mama.

She nodded her consent.

I took a deep breath and slid in next to the two old and now reunited friends.

The whispers and backward glances intensified.

I stared straight ahead, trying to ignore the growing heat in my cheeks.

Mary slid in next to me followed by Mama holding Magdalena.

It was communion Sunday again. This time, when Pastor Troyer passed the bread, Grandma Clara broke a piece off for Aunt Lydia before passing the bread to me.

Gasps and more urgent whispers followed.

Martha turned around and looked at me. *What must she think of me? Have I lost my dearest friend?* Nervous, I bit my lip and then gave her a tremulous smile.

She smiled back.

29
The Letter

"Girls, we must leave soon," Mama called up the stairs. It was time for the church's spring frolic.

Mary stood in front of the looking glass and rubbed her cheeks to bring in some color. "How do I look?"

"Benjamin Hostetler won't be able to take his eyes off of you." I sat on the bed, waiting for her to finish preening.

She smiled as her cheeks glowed even pinker.

Benjamin Hostetler had traveled all the way from New Market just to see her, and Mary invited him to the frolic. He was to stay a week with his cousins in Harrisonburg.

Mary took one last glance in the mirror. "It's still hard to believe Papa has allowed him to court me after all."

"You will probably be married to him in two summers' time."

"Oh, that seems so far away!"

"Time passes swiftly if you keep busy, and you are always busy."

She turned from her reflection and looked at me with a mischievous grin. "Maybe you'll meet someone new tonight, and we will have a double wedding."

I blanched. "No thank you. I am going to be a teacher. Maybe I won't marry at all."

Sister Brubaker will become Mrs. Tobias Miller later this month, a June wedding. In April, the school board asked me to take her place as the school's teacher. I already had so many ideas, things I'd learned from helping my younger brothers with their schoolwork.

Afternoon sunlight bathed the neatly groomed churchyard. Groaning, I settled on the church steps next to Martha. As always, my stomach was stuffed after the congregation's potluck supper. "I shouldn't have had that piece of blackberry pie."

"You had to because you made it," Martha replied. "You have to at least try what you bring, or else how will you know if it was any good?"

Crack! The sound of the bat hitting the ball and the cheers of the crowd drew my attention to the baseball game on the school grounds next to the church. At Peter and Leon's urging, Papa Jacob had sought Brother Troyer's blessing to hold a baseball game at the spring frolic.

"This is fun." Martha nodded her head toward the game. "I'm glad Brother Troyer and the elders gave permission."

I clapped and cheered as Leon raced to first base. "It didn't look like they would at first, but they said they couldn't find the sin in it simply because it is something new."

"Nice hit, Leon," called Papa Jacob from his position as catcher.

"*Danke*, Papa," Leon yelled back.

We all called him Papa now. Magdalena had from the beginning, and the rest of us warmed up to it over time. I still preferred to call him Papa Jacob. My memories of my first father were still too fresh to think of anyone except him as only *Papa*.

Now Brother Troyer was up to bat. Papa Jacob left his spot as catcher and walked over to

Peter who was pitching. He put his arm around Peter and said something to him. Peter nodded and laughed. His anger and mistrust had faded over the past few months. One day in early April, he and Papa Jacob drove to New Market together, only the two of them, and things seemed different after they returned. The light was back in Peter's eyes, and he smiled easily again.

Aunt Lydia sat with Grandma Clara and a few other women near third base, watching the players. Skip sat nearby with a cluster of older men, his contented smile besmeared with blackberry pie. Our family's public acceptance of Aunt Lydia seemed to soften the hearts of the others until little by little, she became a full participant of our congregation. The church members are still careful not to talk about her work, and we are careful not to reveal our involvement. The fewer who know, the safer we all are.

We arrived home after dark. "Children, get to bed as soon as you can. We have church services in the morning," Mama said.

"*Ja*, Mama." Peter yawned and headed upstairs, the other boys following.

I took Magdalena's hand. "Come."

Papa Jacob stopped me. "Wait, Susanna. Let Mary take Magdalena."

Mary looked at me quizzically. I shrugged in response. She took Magdalena's hand and led her upstairs.

"This arrived yesterday." Papa Jacob handed me a letter. "I did not want to give it to you until after the frolic in case it contains bad news."

I looked at the return address. It simply said "Alice" with no last name, and penned underneath was "Montreal, Quebec, Canada."

"Thank you," I whispered. My fingers trembled as I opened it.

May 19, 1850

Dear Susanna,

I am safe in Montreal. We met with some trouble in Delaware but were spared by the Lord's mercy.

Montreal is very cold, but I am well. Mama and I share an apartment with another family. It is crowded but suits our needs at the present time.

George and I found work in a factory. Mama has not been well. She grieves for Lewis. Please reply with any information you may have regarding his welfare.

Someday I pray we meet again. If not on earth, then in a better place.

Sincerely,
Alice
(as dictated to Judith Winston, friend)

I let out a deep breath and looked up at Mama standing next to me. "She's safe." I handed the letter to her to read.

"Thank the Lord," she said.

I took the letter up to Mary and sat on the bed next to her as she scanned the contents. "You need to write her back. Let her know Lewis survived."

"How do I tell her he lost his leg?"

"She doesn't need to know that. Tell her he was sold to a kind family."

That was true. Albert had inquired of Lewis's fate. After Lewis had healed from his injury, his master sold him to a family living in Frederick County at the north end of the state. He was a kitchen boy, hobbling around with the aid of crutches. The head cook doted on him, as did the master's wife.

"What should I tell her about Virgil?"

Mary's face blanched. The news of his hanging was as horrifying now as the day we learned of it. "Tell her...tell her he's moved on to a better place, too."

Lying on my side that night, I listened to Mary and Magdalena's steady breathing and envied their ability to sleep. All I thought about was how I would answer Alice's letter. What could I write that would lessen the pain of losing Lewis? Even if he was well cared for, he was still torn from their lives. Most likely they would never see him again. They certainly would never see Virgil. At least not on this earth. As I did every night, I prayed for Alice and her family. My heart heavy, I grieved for the many more thousands of slaves who had been torn from their families.

Lately I'd heard the word "abolitionist" used to describe someone who worked to make slavery illegal. Papa Jacob said the abolitionists were becoming bolder, and conflict was growing between the northern and southern states. Rumors of war scared me, but it seemed far removed. I didn't expect it to happen here in Harrisonburg. If it ever did, at least I'd learned to trust what Grandma Clara said was true: *Sparrows may fall, but God sees each one, and if he cares for them, surely he cares for me.*

I pulled the covers back, careful not to wake my sisters, and tiptoed to the window. Moonlight gleamed on the apple trees lining the garden. A doe was nibbling on the lower hanging leaves of the trees. A fawn with a spotted rump walked beside her, attempting to nurse. I watched them for a moment until something else caught my eye.

My heartbeat quickened. A warm, yellow light flickered in the window of Aunt Lydia's barn loft.

Glossary and Discussion Guide

In the mid-1800s most Mennonites spoke Pennsylvania Dutch. This unique language formed over time from a mix of Germanic dialects combined with a dash of English after these Anabaptist settlers immigrated to the United States, many in Pennsylvania, in the late 1700s and early 1800s.

During the time this story is set, controversy arose in the Amish/Mennonite communities over using Pennsylvania Dutch or speaking English only. Some became fluent in both languages. Some adopted English only and did not pass the language on to their children. Most Amish and Old Order Mennonites chose to keep their traditions and still speak it today.

Glossary

Pennsylvania Dutch words and phrases used in *When Sparrows Fall*:

Abatz	Stop
Ach	Oh
Armes	Poor
Befuddled	Confused
Danke	Thank you
Dimmel	Thunder
Doplich	Clumsy
Dumkopf	Dumb head
Fraa	Woman
Geboren	Born
Gott im himmel	God in Heaven
Greislich	Horrible
Gretzing	Complaining
Grexy	Cranky
Hees	Hot
Ja	Yes
Kalt	Cold
Kind	Child
Kinskind	Grandchild
Outen	Put out
Redd up	Tidy
Rutsching	Squirming
Schnickelfritz	Troublemaker
Schul	School
Schnell	Hurry
Sit sie da do	Sit down
Strobly	Messy (as pertaining to hair)
Tzooker	Candy
VerKrüppelten	Crippled
Was iss los?	What is going on?
Was iss letz	What happened?
Welt	World

Discussion Guide

What was the Underground Railroad? The Underground Railroad wasn't really under the ground, nor was it literally a railroad. It was a network of people who worked together to help fugitive slaves escape to free states in the north and Canada. They worked secretly because it was against the law. That is why it is called "underground." They used railroad terminology to describe the people helping (stationmasters and conductors), the fugitive slaves (passengers), and the safe houses where the escaped slaves hid (stations). The people who volunteered for the Underground Railroad included freeborn blacks, former slaves, and white abolitionists.

What was an abolitionist? An abolitionist was someone who thought slavery was wrong and actively opposed it. Many abolitionists working on the Underground Railroad were Quakers.

What was Virginia's attitude toward slavery? Slavery in the United States began in Virginia in the 1600s. Slavery was free labor for wealthy plantation owners in the southern states. If they could force people to work their crops without having to pay them, they would make more money. Their prosperity and way of life was dependent upon slave labor. They wanted to keep their slaves and fought for that right during the Civil War.

What was the Fugitive Slave Act? The Fugitive Slave Act, passed in 1850, enacted harsher penalties for those who helped slaves escape to freedom. They could spend six months in jail or be ordered to pay a $1,000 fine (that would be about $28,000 today). It also allowed slave hunters to legally catch runaway slaves in the northern states.

Who are the Mennonites? Mennonites are people who follow Jesus Christ through the teachings of Menno Simons, an Anabaptist religious leader who lived in Friesland (now known as the Netherlands) in the late 1400s and early 1500s. "Anabaptist" means "re-baptize." They believe that people should be allowed to make their own decisions about baptism; consequently, Anabaptists choose not to baptize their babies, and those who have already been baptized as infants are baptized again. The government-backed church leaders in the European nations where Anabaptism began considered rebaptism heresy and heavily persecuted them. In response, many of them fled to the United States for religious freedom. The Amish are cousins of Mennonites, sharing the same roots. They broke apart in 1693 because the Amish believed Mennonites had become too worldly and because of a disagreement about how to discipline straying church members.

Who are the Quakers? Quakers are also Anabaptists, sharing the core values of Mennonites, but their roots are in England.

Quakers formed in the mid-1600s, led by a preacher named George Fox. Like the Mennonites in other parts of Europe, the Quakers were persecuted by the powerful government-backed church and fled to the United States for religious freedom.

How did Mennonites and Quakers feel about slavery? Mennonites refused to own slaves and excommunicated (kicked out) any church members who did. In the late 1600s some Mennonites joined the Quaker church, and together they formed a new town near Philadelphia called Germantown. The Quakers traditionally owned slaves, but many of them were influenced by the example set by their Mennonite friends. In 1688 Mennonites and Quakers joined forces to draft the *1688 Germantown Quaker Petition Against Slavery* to convince other Quakers to free their slaves. The Quakers not only freed their slaves, but they became leaders in the abolitionist movement and active supporters and participants in the Underground Railroad.

Mennonites, on the other hand, believed strongly in the separation of church and state. To them, this meant that they were not to be involved in politics, the military, or social change. Although they viewed slavery as wrong, they also considered it wrong to engage in the "worldly" activities of the Underground Railroad. To do so risked being ostracized by their church community. Still, a few courageous Mennonites decided to take that risk and became involved in the Underground Railroad.

Runaway slave advertisements used in *When Sparrows Fall*:

The first advertisement was originally written by Albert C. Pulliam and placed in the *Daily Dispatch* (a Richmond, Virginia, publication) on April 26, 1861. Names, places, and dates are changed, and the advertisement is condensed. It appears in the Perseus Digital Library from Tufts University. It is licensed for use under the Creative Commons Attribution-Sharealike 3.0 United States License: http://creativecommons.org/licenses/by-sa/3.0/us/legalcode. The second advertisement fits the common style of the time but is completely fictional.

A word about domestic violence: When someone hurts a family member or someone who lives in the same home, it's called abuse or domestic violence, and it's wrong. With the right help, people can learn to manage their anger in ways that do not hurt others. If you or someone you know is hurt at home, you can tell a teacher or call 1-800-799-SAFE. Somebody who cares will keep you safe while giving the person who hurt you the chance to learn better ways of handling anger.

Acknowledgments

Many thanks to the members of my critique group, Debby Zigenis-Lowry, a gifted writer who gives excellent feedback; Tracy Snyder who makes me laugh and writes compelling science fiction; and Beverly Brainard, the Bible scholar, for her gracious hosting. Their expectation of a new chapter every month kept me going. I enjoyed listening to the next chapter in their stories each month. Jessica Johnson was only part of our group for a short time before she moved, but she continues to encourage me from a distance.

Thank you to everyone at Leap Books, starting with Kat O'Shea, my first editor, for seeing its potential in the beginning and for all her advice and encouragement. Thank you to my Leap Books editors, Shannon Delany and Judith Graves, and to three women whom I've never met, but they each helped edit the manuscript through its stages of development: Allison Scoles, Kelly Hashway, and Heather Elia.

I appreciate my connections to Harrisonburg, Virginia: Lois Bowman B. Bowman, librarian at the Menno Simons Historical Library at Eastern Mennonite University in Harrisonburg; my former sophomore English teacher now living in Harrisonburg, Shirley Yoder Brubaker, encouraged me as a writer when I was fifteen; Eric Martin inspired me with photographs he took while on a bike trip through the Shenandoah Valley and also told me about someone named Petunia, who made her way into the story.

Thank you to my co-workers for their encouragement, especially to Dottie Kamilos, the librarian at the school where I teach, for supporting me not just with this book but in so many other ways through the years.

My precious family deserves many thanks (and hugs and kisses): my husband, Alan, for believing in me and for helping me with the technical aspects of the river crossing scene; my oldest son, Mitchell, a talented writer himself, who read my first chapter when he was twelve and wanted to know what would happen next and for helping me come up with the title; my youngest son, Isaac, for giving honest feedback about the cover when it wasn't quite right yet and for giving me space and time to write; my dad, Roy Blackstone, for his constant love and for taking me to the library when I was growing up; and my sister and nieces, Karen, Leesha, and Cera Kropf for showing me what resilience looks like.

To my late mother, and to my Stutzman aunts and uncles and cousins: Yes, I was thinking about you when I wrote this. I love you all. Although this is largely a work of fiction, you might recognize some familiar family dynamics. I wanted you to have a happy ending, so I wrote you one.

Most of all, I thank my Heavenly Father, the giver of all good gifts, who counts the very hairs on our heads and loves us far more than the sparrows. I thank Him for the gifts of writing and imagination.

About Diana Blackstone

Diana has been a voracious reader since age nine when she discovered *The Chronicles of Narnia* after a librarian handed her the first book in the series. She credits hay fever for her interest in writing stories. Unable to play outside without misery from the age of ten, she spent half of every summer vacation inside reading and writing stories until the pollen count dwindled.

Diana serves as a high school English teacher and academic support coordinator. She originally chose to teach older students because she thought they would be able to manage their own bodily fluids better than little kids would. She's discovered she was mostly right about that, and as a bonus, she finds teenagers a blast to spend her days with.

She lives in the Pacific Northwest with her husband Alan and youngest son Isaac. Her adult son Mitchell lives only a four-hour drive away, but Diana wishes it was four minutes instead. She has two cats. Her Maine Coon named Mister Mistoffelees weighs twenty pounds. He is as sweet as he is huge. The other is a feisty Siamese-mix named Sabrina.

Visit Diana at www.dianablackstone.com.

More from Leap Books!

From NYT Bestselling author Maria V. Snyder comes
STORM WATCHER

Lightning never strikes twice, does it?

The youngest son in a family of search-and-rescue dog trainers, Luke must face his deathly fear of storms to prove that he and the dog he's training belong in the family business.

978-1-61603-033-9

Patrice Lyle's
THE CASE OF THE INVISIBLE WITCH

Thirteen-year-old Tulip Bonnaire, Witch PI, runs Spells & Spies out of her dorm room at Poison Ivy Charm School, a school for polite witches and warlocks. She only has 72 hours to figure out her latest case, or her classmate Missy will never be seen again.

978-1-61603-034-6

Bonnie J. Doerr's
ISLAND STING

When city girl Kenzie Ryan moves to a wildlife refuge, she plunges straight into an eco-mystery. Kenzie trades New York streets for Florida Keys pollution cleanup, and now instead of hailing cabs, she's tracking down a poacher of endangered Key deer!

978-1-61603-002-5

Bonnie J. Doerr's
STAKEOUT

A haunting promise compels Kenzie to ensure sea turtle survival by ending a rash of nest robberies. Fearless wheelchair-bound Ana and savvy troubled Angelo assist Kenzie in an undercover sting that grows increasingly complicated and treacherous.

978-1-61603-007-0

For more exciting books from Leap, visit
www.LeapBks.com.

Meet our authors, read our blog—LEAP into great stories and new worlds!